Thanksgiving Leads
to Christmas: A Daybook

Elaine Eachus

AuthorHouse™ LLC
1663 Liberty Drive
Bloomington, IN 47403
www.authorhouse.com
Phone: 1-800-839-8640

Published by AuthorHouse 09/20/2013

ISBN: 978-1-4918-1165-8 (sc)
ISBN: 978-1-4918-1167-2 (e)

Library of Congress Control Number: 2013915492

This book is printed on acid-free paper.

authorHOUSE®

Thanksgiving Leads to Christmas is for my family, without whom this story is incomplete. I have been loved and learned so much from each of you. To Andy and Tim, our sons, Lyn and Beth, our daughters-in-law, and the six wonders of the world, our grandchildren, Robert, Victoria, Jackson, Ashley, Elizabeth, and Emily, thank you for being in my life.

This book is also dedicated to my nieces and nephews with whom I share so much history. I have grateful memories of my siblings, Donna, Alice, and James, my parents and in-laws, aunts and uncles, all saints in time now. Your lives are in these pages.

Special thanks go to my husband, Alan, or "Ace" as I call him, for unfailing support and encouragement on this long journey. Your help is in every page as I trudged through the process.

Contents

Introduction...3

Thursday, November 28 *Putting Away Grandma's Dishes* 4

Friday, November 29 *Blue and Purple Blues*...5

Saturday, November 30 *And He Shall Be Called* 7

Sunday, December 1 *TLC: Thanksgiving Leads to Christmas*.......................9

Monday, December 2 *Something Sweet*...12

Tuesday, December 3 *Prayer for an Advent Morning* 13

Wednesday, December 4 *Elizabeth's Tree* 14

Thursday, December 5 *Beauty, How Like a Rose, Late Bloomer*..................16

Friday, December 6 *St. Nicholas Day* 18

Saturday, December 7 *Annunciation* 19

Sunday, December 8 *TLC: Too Little Currency*...20

Monday, December 9 *Making Truffles* 23

Tuesday, December 10 *Human Rights Day* 25

Wednesday, December 11 *Holiday Traffic*..26

Thursday, December 12 *The Forgiveness Piece* 29

Friday, December 13 *St. Lucia Day*...31

Saturday, December 14 *Edward and the Language of Love* 33

Sunday, December 15 *TLC: The Long-Distance Call* 35

Monday, December 16 *Christmas Cookies*..38

Tuesday, December 17 *Lucy Lemon Bars* 41

Wednesday, December 18 *The Present*...42

Thursday, December 19 *By George* 44

Friday, December 20 *An Evening with the Angels* 47

Saturday, December 21 *Blue Christmas*...49

Sunday, December 22 *TLC: Tangled, Loving Circles* 51

Monday, December 23 *The Sled* 53

Tuesday, December 24 *Long Ago Star* 56

Wednesday, December 25 *Lullaby for Christmas* 58

Introduction

A few years ago I decided I wanted to write a story for each of my grandchildren. I wrote about Christmas. As a wife, mother, teacher, pastor, and grandmother, I know that Christmas is a place for love to spill into our hearts and out to nurture us and others in unimagined and mystical ways. Never having known my grandparents, I wrote for the parts in our lives that feel lonely or unnoticed in the frenzy of the season. Through the years and through many Christmases I have discovered that what we think is missing may be discovered as love wrapped in different packaging. I hope that day by day in this Advent season each of us can move toward the place where love blooms full in our hearts.

Several years before I began this adventure, a dear friend who is my spiritual director, Dr. Martha Bartholomew, encouraged me to start writing seriously. Age and time have wonderful ways of giving answers to the why questions of existence. This is my offering because I may and because I must. Profound thanks to Martha for her inspiration and for her modeling of life as a Follower of the Way.

I am indebted to Dr. Martha Bartholomew for her unfailing guidance and support, to Dr. Nancy Moore for her constructive and supportive help with the manuscript, to Dr. Paul Stiffler and Elsie Stiffler who have read and offered their accumulated insights, to Louise Brodie who arranged my songs, and to Leonard Farina for proofreading the manuscript. Your help was invaluable as I wove stories of my life with the fantasy of my heart and imagination into my offering of thankfulness.

My thankfulness continues as the royalties from this book will go to the Back Bay Mission in Biloxi, Mississippi where I have learned thankfulness from those who have suffered much and are so truly grateful.

There are reminders in Thanksgiving that lead us to deeper reflections of who we are and what we are celebrating. Our families are launching pads to journeys of acceptance and perspectives that can lead us to wonder, delight, and even thankfulness.

Putting Away Grandma's Dishes

I'm compulsive. It's midnight.

Thanksgiving needs to be tied up. Otherwise how can Christmas come?

Extended family left at nine, kids out with friends, napkins and tablecloth now

Jumbled like kittens looking for the softest spot in the laundry basket.

Silverware washed, carefully dried, set on the counter,

Grandma's Bavarian bone china, with the gold edge and blue cornflowers

Sits on the dining room table, awaiting the white, quilted plastic coffins

Where it will rest undisturbed.

Nine descendants and three strays brought together by happenstance, tradition,

And loneliness consumed truffle-stuffed turkey and cranberry chipotle chutney,

And Grandma's ghost shook her head in dismay as poached pears in cream and kirsch

Brought down the extravaganza to recall the blessings of simple.

We love those minutely detailed dishes, but Grandma wouldn't be happy.

She would rant about excess on the day to celebrate survival amid adversity,

So what's the big deal about her dishes? Portable, easily put away, point to another reality,

Harboring truths of our DNA etched between diminutive sprays—our deepest reflections match.

Hurrah for Grandma's dishes. We didn't break a one.

Now zipped up in their cocoons, we have twenty-eight days to prepare

For the next encounter when truest simplicity breaks into our midst—

I must plan my attack.

Preparing for Christmas can feel like a race in many directions. It's hard to know where to start, much less how to reach the destination. Before Advent we look at the churches' altar guilds preparing their sanctuaries and find they, too, are on different paths to Christmas.

Blue and Purple Blues

Tactile technicians assemble. Advent's almost here,

Blue paraments outed by the Anglicans.

Presbyterians swathe the chancel in purple, looking inward at our sin,

While at St. Thomas they parse seasonal correctness no matter the color.

At St. Paul's UCC the ancient pastor gets out his red stole,

Claims he loves Christmas red.

Blue and purple with a dash of red—what color for a baby's bed?

Pondering Presbyterians, Catholics, UCC, and the Anglicans

Can't decide what my Christmas preparations might be,

So many pressures, so many choices, can't make up my mind.

Blue and purple with a dash of red, haunted, searching, what will *I* find?

Now I have tried with sincerity to be in the zone for the Lord's nativity.

Journey to Bethlehem is a rutted road and large deceptive signs insure

Not many will reach the royal city, nor cradle David's heir.

Blue and purple with a dash of red, made some crazy detours, went someplace else instead.

So here's to Anglican purity and the Presbyterians' penitential call.

UCC cries justice; St. Thomas assured, but fingering frayed edges,

Trial and error on the threaded course, I lament.

Blue and purple with a dash of red, don't know where I'm going, don't know *if* I'm sent.

God of so many Advents, watch over those lost, wandering souls

Whose days—all winter solstices, whose nights—wombs sloshing in uncertainty,

Let their muffled cries become prayers of welcome for One who waited in eternity's wings

To dance in blue and purple with a dash of red, mundane places where He lays his head.

My spiritual director reminded me that in the book of Exodus Moses received instructions from God as to how the Israelites are to worship in the Promised Land. In chapters 35 through 39 we hear instructions that blue, purple, and crimson yarns and fine twisted linen are to be used for the curtains in the temple.

And He Shall Be Called

We got to the airport on time that December morning although the snush, snow and slush, was freezing fast-forming cavernous ruts on the side streets that hit the underbody of the car with tremendous thunks if you tried to cross one of its ridges. We figured we'd have to wait for them to deice the plane. Not to worry. We had plenty of time.

This was a journey of great importance. Our son had finished an advanced degree on his own, and tonight he was graduating with so many others at this blue-collar university in Detroit. He had completed this while he was working at a bank after he had graduated from college. He began his gradual ascent from teller to loan officer. He had sandwiched in this degree around sports, his first love, and moving many, many times as young people do just starting out. But he had done it entirely on his own, and as parents we were proud of his accomplishment.

When we arrived at the airport, we scanned the departure board and noted the flight was delayed, so my husband and I headed to the lounge for frequent flyers and settled down with the *Tribune* and a cup of coffee. We had read the paper, finished a second cup of coffee, and still the board showed no departure time. Heading back to the grazing area, I spotted Mohammed Ali seated by himself and rushed back to tell my husband. I remembered him as "Float like a butterfly, sting like a bee" Cassius Clay. What a spark of excitement and enthusiasm he brought to boxing! What fun it would be to give our son Mohammed Ali's autograph. He turned down the offer of paper and instead laboriously wrote his greeting on a piece of Black Muslim literature. The great fighter was as patient with himself while he labored to write his name as he had been with our request that interrupted his work.

When we asked at the desk, we were told the whole Midwest was having weather-related problems, so lunch became an apple and some crackers shared with others checking out the snacks with one eye peeled at the departure board. We were beginning to get a little worried, for we feared if the traffic were tied up in Detroit, we might not make it to the Renaissance Center in time for graduation. Oh yes, I had just the outfit for graduation in my suitcase, so I wanted to check into the hotel beforehand. It was going to be tight—the time, not the outfit.

It was after two o'clock when we finally boarded the plane, and with an hour's time difference we knew we would have to rush to get the car and get to graduation. Rush we did, and we arrived just in time to make it into the cavernous auditorium before the music started. The speaker, a former graduate himself, told the graduates to never be ashamed of their alma mater, for many before them and many who would come after them would make contributions—some great, some small—to move their communities forward in time's relentless march. "It is what you do with the tools of your degree that will be your mark on the world," he said.

Andy, our son, had earned his MBA. We took him out that night to a restaurant where he had worked as a valet to earn tuition money, and we ate every kind of raw oyster on the menu. He graciously spent the evening with us instead of going out with his friends to celebrate. His friends knew him as Don, for when he moved to Detroit after college, he decided that Andy didn't conjure up a mature enough image because he still looked like a sixteen-year-old. Don, he explained, was a more mature-sounding name.

The next day we three headed out to Greenfield Village to see the cars, the Cotswold Cottages, and the craftsmen practicing crafts centuries old. Groundskeepers with frozen hands were putting up Christmas decorations in the snow-topped yesteryear. We bought a star at the gift shop like the one the tinsmith had made in his shop. We drank lots of hot chocolate and marveled at the extent of Henry Ford's vision and the depth of his pocketbook to bring so many historic buildings together in Dearborn. That day, my husband and son indulged me in all the charm of Americana that I love. On the way back to our son's apartment we bought some sugar cookie dough in a tube and three ingredients for frosting and tried cutting out Christmas cookies by gently patting a slice of dough into a big enough circle to cut our Greenfield Village star. It was a rudimentary and messy process, but it felt like Christmas!

Sunday was one of those mornings when a million diamonds glistened in the snow and the whole world was decked in brightness. My husband and I headed for McDonald's, as we were sure Andy would prefer sleep to breakfast. We sat among the older ladies who had come after mass and the families with kids bouncing like they were in the TV commercials wanting everything sweet on the menu. We had some time to kill before we picked up Andy for church.

At the window I noticed a man sitting by himself, smoking a cigarette. He sat there as people came and left. I realized he wasn't waiting for anyone and hadn't ordered anything. Uncharacteristically I left my husband and started talking to a stranger. "Breakfast was good this morning. My husband and I had pancakes. I was wondering if you would like to try something like that." We negotiated what he would like, and I went to the counter.

I set the tray in front of him and told him I hoped he would enjoy it. He asked me my name. I told him. "You know," he began, "my mother named me Immanuel. She told me what it meant, but I forgot."

"I think I can help you out," I said, recalling that this was the first Sunday in Advent, the time to begin preparing our hearts and lives for the birth of Jesus. "Your name means God with us."

He thought about that for a while and said, "I am going to remember that."

I don't recall anything the minister said or did that Sunday morning, the first Sunday in Advent in Detroit. I don't remember leaving Andy that afternoon. But my preparation for Christmas had begun with a man, Cassius Clay (Mohammed Ali), writing a greeting slowly, laboriously, and with great dignity for our son, Don (Andy), who made Christmas cookies with his parents. I remembered the words of the prophet Isaiah, "Look, the young woman is with child and shall bear a son, and shall name him Immanuel, God with us." *Yes*, I thought as I settled in for the hour flight home, *God is with us.*

TLC: Thanksgiving Leads to Christmas

A Sermon for the First Sunday in Advent

Here we are! We have finally crossed the threshold of the long-anticipated days of merchants, Black Friday, and shop locally Saturday. Cyber Monday is tomorrow. With Thanksgiving a fading memory of fabulous food, we make a commitment to renewed dietary and physical health in the forthcoming season. We march forth like runners at the Chicago marathon, some carefully pacing themselves, some hanging back to let others fall and fail in front of them before their sprint to Christmas, but we are all here at the starting line of the holiday marathon.

The energized already have their lights up outside, their tree trimmed, and some truly inspired have their cards addressed. Some are waiting for the infusion of Christmas spirit to enter this countdown to Christmas. But every year we look ahead, some as wide-eyed children, some as weary pilgrims, some with resolute determination and careful pacing to reach Christmas morning standing. But before the games begin, we need to look over our shoulders to see from where we have come.

Too Busy for Thankfulness

When our younger son became engaged to Beth on Columbus Day weekend, he told his future bride that they were going to enjoy their engagement, the here and now of it for at least a month. There would be no planning a wedding, just enjoyment of this moment in their lives. Laughing, he asked, "You know how long that lasted, don't you?" We live in an urgent society of scarcity. *We had better hurry up, and get it or somebody else might get it first.* News reports tell us what toys and video games to grab first as they are hot items this year. Florists, caterers, and bakeries already have the appointment books bulging with those who carefully plan for the holiday season to make it the best ever! We often believe the hype that there won't be anything left for us if we don't hurry. We have cause for thankfulness, however, because Tim and Beth have been married many years.

The Sinking Sensation

Strangely some of us will wake up the twenty-sixth of December with the sinking sensation that what remains of Christmas will be revived in January when our credit card bills arrive. Some of us will be aware of how bone-weary we are from all the business and busyness of the season. Some will awake with a faint sense of disappointment that some part of Christmas we had invested ourselves in this year just didn't meet our hopes, or some gift we had so thoughtfully and carefully selected didn't meet expectations. Some will arise to the disquieting feeling that there was still something missing from the mix even after they gave Christmas their best shot, some longing yet to be fulfilled.

So on this Sunday, let's look back. George Santayana said, "Those who ignore their history are doomed to repeat it." Socrates said at his trial for heresy, "The unexamined life is not worth living." Let's sit on the log with Socrates and Santayana and examine what's been happening. The first American Thanksgiving was a celebration in the midst of devastating loss and few guarantees for survival for our forebears at the Plymouth Plantation. There had been huge costs; exactly half of their number had died that first year. Yet with the help of Squanto, who spoke English, they learned how to live with few provisions, and they also learned some hunting and fishing through that interminable winter during which death stalked the Pilgrims and many fell. Yet God's people survived. They undoubtedly remembered those whom they had lost during that first difficult year, but they also saw how God had been with them. Their Thanksgiving was a celebration of thankfulness, a multicultural feast with those who had helped them endure.

A Living Thanksgiving

A Confederate soldier during the Civil War came to thankfulness through the privations of war. He wrote that of all the things he had asked God to give him he had not been given, but had received the seeming opposite. In the gifts God had given, the soldier found the greatest blessing and made him a man richly blessed.

So it was with Job. Through no fault of his own, he lost his riches, family, and health. Even his friends who came to console the despairing wretch suggested that somehow he or his wild children were responsible for the catastrophe in which he now lived. Yet even Job, even in his suffering, remembered to be thankful. He told his wife, who suggested he should curse God and die, "Shall we receive the good at the hand of God, and not receive the bad?" (Job 2:10). Like Socrates and the Confederate soldier, Job understood it was in the opposite extreme that we could see glimmers of our true blessings. Part of this TLC, "Thanksgiving Leads to Christmas," is seeing in the simple acts of thankfulness that we are reaching out to take God's hand in a way that may seem counterintuitive to the images of Christmas our merchants, magazines, and media present.

Then why do we forget to say, "Thank you," so frequently? Could it be that we begin to assume that we are in charge? Without a measure of grace, we continue our fantasy of subduing and conquering our circumstances—in this case the rush to Christmas. But with our thankfulness we can enter in others' joys and suffering instead of using others as comparisons to see how well our Christmas is progressing.

It Takes Practice

True thankfulness is a discipline. Want to be a disciple of the peasant boy of Palestine? Then practice thankfulness. Watch those whom you admire spread thankfulness like peanut butter slathered on bread. It is the beginning of growing into the amazing newness of life that God has for us. Those who go on mission trips around the country and around the world hear, "Thank you so much. Thank you for coming." Roger Dart, the United Church of Christ pastor who led mission trips several times a year to rebuild in New Orleans after Katrina, says he believes that those who have lost so much in the material sense have a spiritual understanding of thankfulness. They recognize what little power and control they have in rebuilding their lives in a city where 28 percent of the population live below the poverty level. They have learned how to be grateful for the blessings of waking each morning in God's care, and they wait patiently—even years—to rebuild their homes. They have learned that thankfulness begets thankfulness and a true relationship of created and creator. They have learned that speaking our thanks gives us life beyond what we are able to effect. It changes us and our relationships.

Thankful In and For Tough Times

It is not a sugar-coated treat, although sometimes when we are its recipient, it is so unexpected and sweet it brings tears to our eyes. Thankfulness is hard work. As Job reminds us, we are to be thankful in all of life's circumstances. We may be standing in the difficult valleys where there are no green pastures and the still waters are all dried up. We haven't seen the good shepherd in miles, and night is descending rapidly. Here is not where we expect to find ourselves experiencing gratitude. Our cry is more like the prophet Isaiah's, "O that you would tear open the heavens and come down, so that the mountains would quake at your presence" (Isaiah 64:1). Our lives seem to be in shambles; our souls ache. But TLC, "Thanksgiving Leads to Christmas," is that spiritual work. Those who have journeyed to Bethlehem began their thankful lists with the easy parts, things and relationships that worked well and for which they were profoundly grateful.

Then there are other parts, the thorny parts of our lives, where it is hard to imagine gratitude; they simply cause pain and draw blood. But making thankfulness lists every day is helpful. They are not another thing to be checked off like getting stamps at the post office. Thankfulness is a daily list to be lived, imagining how God is present in both the good and the difficult situations. Writing things down moves our burdens from deep inside us where they can feel knotted and constricted to a more manageable space where we can look at them with a modicum of dispassion. That distance from inside to outside can bring perspective and balance and a new sense of proportion to heavy burdens. Outside we can see it in a larger context. Written down, we can return to it and see other parts of our lives in relationship to our pain. Written down, we can feel our burden as a part of who we are, but not all of us.

Being Thankful Together

Look at the Psalms, the hymn book of the Hebrews. Psalm 80 recalls that Shepherd of Israel had saved them and even brought them out of bondage, but right now all they felt was God's anger—a bread of tears and a cup of salty water. The psalm ends with the prayer, "Restore us, O Lord God of hosts; let your face shine, that we may be saved" (Isaiah 80:10).

The Hebrews used the liturgy to express their deepest feelings … in community. Reciting the psalm, the whole community could remember and relate to the times when they had experienced the same reality. But in the middle of the mess, they could recall that this "mess" was the beginning of the message. We know that. We have often been strengthened when our deepest feelings have been acknowledged—neither judged nor psychologized, just acknowledged. We are changed when we acknowledge our thankfulness, when we express our deepest gratitude to others. Our center becomes attuned to unrecognized blessings that often reside in the midst of our pain.

Start your thanksgiving list. Then pray it. One pastor I know would open a page of her church directory when she got in her car. Before she started to drive, she would read the names of all the parishioners in one column. As she drove, she would pray for them, thankful that they were part of her community. Praying our thankful list moves our hearts into this season of expectancy. There are revelations still to be made. There are lessons that we need to learn or relearn. Socrates and Santayana are still on the log, talking of how the past can shape a more meaningful today. The Holy Spirit is waiting to bring calmness to our anxious spirits and acceptance to our unyielding circumstances. May we live into the reality of our faith and hope. Amen.

Something Sweet

When our Pilgrim forebears came to America, there were stern admonitions against frivolity and celebration of our Lord's birth, and punishments meted out. The Pilgrims' pastor, John Robinson, said, "It seems too much for any mortal man to appoint, or make anniversary memorial" for Christ. Fortunately he also said, "God has yet more light and truth to break forth out of his holy Word." Five hundred years later and we are definitely into Christmas. The struggle is how to make an appropriate memorial for God breaking into our world. So whether Advent catches us in Mary's humility or the need to repent of too much material Christmas, small quantities of something sweet can bring joy to our journey.

3 1/4 lbs. fully ripe pears, enough to make 4 cups; peeled, pitted and finely chopped

Zest of one lemon

Juice of one lemon, about 2 T. juice

2/3 cup crystallized ginger, chopped

1 box natural fruit pectin, 1.75 oz.

1/2 t. butter

5 c. sugar

12 4-ounce fruit jars with lids and rings

Ginger Pear Marmalade

Assemble all equipment and ingredients. Put 5 cups of sugar in a separate bowl. Wash, peel, and core pears. Chop the fruit in small bits but not a mush. Measure 4 cups of fruit into a 6- or 8-quart saucepan. Stir lemon juice, zest, crystallized ginger, pectin, and butter into the prepared fruit. Bring marmalade mixture to a full rolling boil on high heat. A rolling boil is one that doesn't stop when stirred vigorously. Dump sugar in all at once. Stir well and keep stirring until mixture comes to a full rolling boil again and boil for one minute exactly. Immediately remove from heat and skim off any foam. Ladle into hot sterilized fruit jars, filling to 1/8 inch of the top of the jar and process according to manufacturers' direction in a hot water bath for ten minutes.

From start to the removal of the jars of marmalade from the hot water bath, it takes one hour after you have assembled all your ingredients. Cool completely, wash jars to remove any residue, and label. You might want to use your jars of marmalade on St. Nicholas' Day, December 6.

Prayer for an Advent Morning

When morning gilds the sky today and rosy fingers again reveal earth in tumultuous
disarray with
war a car bomb away,
hunger leading to starvation following genocide, lust, power,
and greed.

When morning gilds the sky today and snow blankets a December morning,
covering the dull ache of too many choices,
our desire to think we can have it all, do it all.
Be perfect however we would spell it, our eyes are shrouded and dull.

When morning gilds the sky today and one prays for sanity amid the cascading
images of a distorted past, another screams in silent mistrust, while
frantic and frenetic, we hurry to the next good thing one, unable to go any farther,
traces the river of life flowing in her palm.

When morning gilds the sky
notices
traces
wonders

a spot of sunlight moves slowly across worn carpet.

The cat stretches and moves to its warmth.

Elizabeth's Tree

As I hurried home from the frame shop, I couldn't wait to unwrap the small package. I had promised my husband we would share it together. We had had the treasure for a long time. But every Christmas since we started spending the winters here, we would arrive right before Christmas, and there hadn't been time to get it framed before the holiday. This year we had come early. I imagined it hanging right by the kitchen door. No, maybe it would be better in the hall.

My husband was deep in thought at his computer as I marched inside. Retirement has given us both time to realize how precious grandchildren are. He especially is devoted to all things grandchild. We travel long distances to witness ballet recitals, babysit for children to give parents a night or weekend away, or have a week with the family on a resort where hopefully we can be together and enjoy the beach, a favorite for all our grandchildren, and cousins can get to know each other. I held up the trophy as I entered his office.

Tearing off the brown paper, my husband joined me as we looked at the Crayola drawing on light blue paper. There was Elizabeth's drawing, made when she was five or six. Elizabeth and I had sat at her table, and we had colored and talked. The table was in the family dining room, which then held kid furniture and a corner hutch filled with art supplies and children's books. She loved to draw. Her lefty style turned out picture after picture. On that day right before sharing Thanksgiving, we sat at her table and chatted about everything and nothing at all. It was a kindergarten girl and her grandmother thinking about Christmas and turning out Christmas images in the forty-eight colors.

Now after five years Elizabeth's Christmas tree resides in a small black frame with a rusty red mat. It is a chubby tree with colored lights of red, blue, mauve pink, and purple, her favorite colors. It sits in a substantial container of rusty brown in the winter snow. Snowflakes fall almost imperceptibly on the palest of bluish gray paper, the way the first lazy snowflakes of winter had fallen in that late afternoon light.

Elizabeth's tree had captured the magic of Christmas. We sat and colored the afternoon away. I remember thinking how much I just loved being able to color with her. Her family had moved away from Chicago that Labor Day. Now we were able to do kid stuff and talk about this and that in her new home in Virginia. That moment was so precious I wished I could remember more. Was she telling me what she hoped Santa would bring her for Christmas, what Mr. Wyman, her kindergarten teacher, was doing with the class, or did we talk about her brother and baby sister?

We gaze at the picture intently. My husband nods approvingly. "It feels like Christmas now," he says. "Sometimes on the farm in Chittenango when Jim and I were growing up, we would put our Christmas tree in a big bucket like Elizabeth drew. We would cut a tree that grew in our woods. We'd put the tree in a twenty-five-pound can that frozen cherries came in, using rocks to hold the tree upright."

I remembered the Christmas when my mother and I went to get a tree at a neighbor's tree farm. It must have been a late afternoon in mid-December, as we didn't put up the tree until a week or so before Christmas. My mother was always glad that I liked putting it up, as she had other things that needed her attention, like making Christmas pajamas for everyone in the family. We walked through the crunching snow to a tree lot a long way from the road. Armed with a bow saw, I was sure that we would find the perfect tree for that Christmas. I think my mother was more pragmatic about the event, but the sight of all these shaped trees and the smell of freshly cut evergreens was more delightful than any candy store for me. As the shadows deepened, we started looking seriously for the perfect tree, and we almost stumbled over a glob of green amid the brown grasses and weeds and wondrous trees. There half hidden under another tree was a six-foot beauty. We wondered aloud if a poacher had been caught and abandoned the endeavor as someone approached. Perhaps, we decided, someone had cut the tree, then had sighted a better one, and had abandoned this one for perfection.

It didn't take my mother long to make an executive decision. She pulled the tree from the other tree and in one swift move set it upright and gave it a spin. "Looks good to me," she said, "and besides it would be a shame to leave the tree here after it has been cut." I pulled the tree through the snow to the road where my mother completed the transaction—five dollars if you cut the tree yourself.

On the weekend my mother and I got the bucket of sand and set the tree in it in the corner of the living room. We poured water into the bucket so the tree could drink all it wanted while it stood bedecked and proud for the festivities. We took a white sheet and tucked it into the top of the bucket, trying to make it look like snow. Big, colored lights like those that Elizabeth had drawn brought joy to the tree, although our lights were orangey gold and white and green and blue and red. The star was a scary creation with a spiral coil that slipped over the topmost spike of the tree, and in a metal white case were five glass triangles, one for each point of the star. In the back was the socket to put a white Christmas bulb. The light illuminated the glass, and it was supposed to make the star seem to sparkle; however, it cast foreboding shadows across the living room ceiling. It never seemed to approximate the glory of the star I imagined guiding men to find the desire of their hearts and longings.

Frustrating globs of aluminum foil cut in long thin strips and sold as icicles were glued together by the manufacturer, which translated into either a very thick mess of icicles thrown on the tree or a long and tedious procedure of trying to separate the strands and then trying to get them to hang over the branches by a small fragment of the strand so the icicles would shimmer in the light. Like Elizabeth's tree we put neither star nor icicles on our tree today, preferring the top of the tree to point to heaven, and as for icicles, they would look out of place in Florida anyway.

That tree rewarded us for our rescue. I remember the pungency of the freshly cut tree permeating our house for the entire season. My mother had been right. It would have been a shame to have left the tree unloved after it had been cut. When Christmas was over, we would take the tree outside and set it up in my mother's snow-topped vegetable garden. She would put suet on it for the birds, and by early spring it would be consigned to the brush pile beyond the garden. Yet trees of Christmas are symbols pointing beyond themselves to realities of our hearts.

Twelfth Night is when the church celebrates the arrival of magi who bring the Prince of Peace strange gifts for a baby, yet fitting for the life that God had given him. We invited friends over to enjoy the final vestiges of Christmas with us before this year's Fraser fir rode to the tree recycling center in town. They are winter residents from Hungary and don't have a Christmas tree as they usually arrive just before Christmas. How our guests enjoyed our tree! They really seemed to appreciate our ornaments that were precious reminders of Christmases past and this year's new ornament from the White House Christmas, a birthday present from Elizabeth and her family.

Art talked about getting an orange for Christmas as a child in Hungary and noticing everything about that orange and what a big deal it was. He was particularly grateful to his godfather, who had given it to him. Art told us he remembered that when he was a small child, they once had had a Christmas tree in their house, but there were many Christmases when there was no tree. Later he remembered getting a branch of evergreen and bringing it home. Times were very difficult in Hungary then. Our tree seemed to transport them to a special place. As they were leaving, I heard Mary say to Art, "We should get a tree next year." I noticed that they were holding hands.

As my husband closed the door, I glanced at Elizabeth's tree on the top of the bookcase, and I wondered what my eleven-year-old granddaughter would one day tell her grandchildren about Christmas trees.

Bringing out Christmas decorations reminds us of special people and special times in our family history. So too, looking back at the beauty of the year deepens our appreciation of this time.

Beauty

What is the beauty of the thing?

Yesterday morning I discovered blue iris blooming by the driveway.

Never bothered to shout or announce it.

They quietly did what iris do. It was enough.

Then rain dotted translucent, gossamer petals.

Iridescence touches unimaginable sheerness.

It was enough.

If iris and raindrop on an ordinary Thursday in May

Could become the eye feast at supper,

Then perhaps for God there is no such thing as ordinary.

How Like a Rose

Like a rose, many petals shaded,

Nuanced, velvet graded,

Cherished in the bud, caressed in

Falling. Some, by accident of garden, are lifted up,

Fragrance imbibed,

Touch both given and received.

Color, cacophonous color, bold and subtle,

Cherished for a day, beauty recalled, imprinted forever.

Late Bloomer

Today in starts and fits

It squalled, rained, sleeted, snowed.

In the courtyard against winter's first tantrum a yellow-leafed willow

Stands scantily clad for today's mewing rage.

Did you notice the weeper hiding slyly behind spring's skirts?

Dropping bare branches she had whipped against winter's mounting snows.

Then sweeping and twirling her slender arms bare she was a dervish of childlike enterprise.

Dancing naked as others dressed for the vernal extravaganza.

But come November when her March shortcoming is but

Forgotten, she reminds others of her season and

Intention not to go gently into that wintry night.

St. Nicholas Day

St. Nicholas, tradition tells us, was born in Myra, which is in present-day Turkey. His father died when Nicholas was young, and he was raised by an uncle who was a bishop of Myra. Nicholas also became a bishop and was tortured during the Roman emperor Diocletian's purge because of his support for the poor. Today we remember St. Nicholas for his gift-giving. One of the acts of kindness attributed to Nicholas was helping a poor man who had three daughters of marrying age. He had no money for their dowries, and if they couldn't marry, they would probably have to support themselves as prostitutes. As the legend goes, as each daughter reached the age of marriage, Nicholas threw a bag of gold through the poor man's window, except for the last daughter. She had washed her stockings and hung them over the embers in the fireplace to dry. Nicholas threw the gold down the chimney, and it landed in her stocking. (Are you beginning to feel a little St. Nick creeping into the story?) Interestingly Nicholas is also a patron saint of pawnbrokers because of the three bags of gold, which became the three gold balls on the pawnbroker's sign.

The Compassionate Bishop

St. Nicholas is also remembered for helping sailors. During a great famine in Myra a ship was in the harbor loaded with wheat for the emperor in Constantinople. Nicholas asked the sailors for wheat for the starving people in Myra. They were reluctant because they knew the wheat had to be delivered and weighed when it reached the emperor. The sailors finally granted Nicholas' request, and to their surprise when they reached the harbor in Constantinople, the grain weighed exactly what it had when it was loaded into the ship's hold. Through Nicholas' request and the sailors' generosity, the people had enough wheat to survive the famine.

In medieval times nuns in Western Europe used St. Nicholas Night to deliver baskets of food and clothes anonymously to the poor. In the Netherlands sailors in harbor towns would have masses and celebrations honoring St. Nicholas, who protected sailors. On the way home they would stop at shops and Nicholas Fairs to buy some presents for their children who had left their shoes outside the door before they had gone to bed.

You be the judge. Are St. Nicholas and Santa Claus intimately related? Just in case they are, let's plan a party remembering the poor. The scale must remain simple. Invite children, family, and friends to celebrate. Ask them to bring a pair of socks to give to a homeless shelter where socks are always in high demand. Or you might take your party to those who might need cheer, an after-care center, an adult day care center, or a soup kitchen.

Ask guests to take off their shoes outside the door. Once everyone has gathered, tell the story of St. Nicholas in your own words. Ask others to share their recollections of St. Nicholas and Santa Claus. Every party needs food, so we will have oranges, which according to legend, St. Nicholas brought to the children in the cold winters of Low Country. Have fun making popcorn balls, and then wrap some to be shared with the recipients of the socks you brought as gifts. Serve hot chocolate to your guests. People enjoy sharing St. Nicholas' generous spirit with others.

Encourage guests to bring CDs or musical instruments for singing the joys of Christmas. A reading of Chris Van Allsburg's *The Polar Express* increases the delight as we hear how Santa gives the "first gift of Christmas" to a small boy. Place wrapped chocolate at each pair of shoes at your door. A jingle bell and ribbon pinned on coats will remind guests to keep the spirit of giving alive in this season.

Annunciation

Somewhere in our "Thanksgiving Leads to Christmas" journey we have to say yes to be pilgrims to the truth, simplicity, and mystery of an Advent journey. What better role model than Mary, who is greeted by an angel bearing a lily in Botticelli's painting "The Annunciation?"

"No thank you, sir, not now," she firmly said.

Slim arms raised in protest, she backs away.

"See, I am dancing. My spirit is led.

Somehow my footsteps are showing the way."

Lily as tribute, he stoops low to greet her.

"This sign will capture the fair maiden's eye."

Halting midstep, her arms twirl in a blur.

Sharp pain from within, then comes a soft sigh.

She sees in his hand God's promise and greeting,

Piercing eyes announce what words couldn't ask.

God's bending to lift us, fruit of this meeting

Consent to God's impossible task.

Many announce in self-contained rooms,

But she brings a baby to smash the earth's gloom.

TLC: Too Little Currency

A Sermon for the Second Sunday in Advent

Where would you begin to tell your Christmas story? What would you say if you turned to the person next to you and started to talk about your Christmas? Would it be with the things you have accomplished on the countdown to Christmas? Would it be the excitement in your children or grandchildren, or the eyes of the kids next door as they twirl like dervishes toward Christmas? Would your Christmas story be tempered with some of the realities of this past year? Part of our charm and a human foible is that we are caught up in the immediacy of our situations. We tend to focus on life lived close to us. Sometimes it is hard to step back and see a broader horizon.

Where Are We Now?

Before the days of a GPS in our automobiles, directions would befuddle me. Sometimes after I tried to understand and repeat back directions from a gas station attendant, I would exclaim, "I don't think I can get there from here!" On our Advent journey we may feel that there is no conceivable way we can do all that we have on our lists before Christmas. Like a ball of yarn and an energetic kitten we can't imagine a beginning or entertain the idea of finding the end. We are literally caught in the now that marks December for many of us.

Sometimes it is comfortable being in that ball of yarn. It keeps us from thinking too much about the deeper stuff. It can keep us from questioning our faith. True Christmas is countercultural. It does not depend on us. Let me repeat that. Christmas does not depend on us. Yet we drive ourselves crazy with expectations and hopes for all the things we might accomplish and do during one month of thirty-one days, of which twenty-five are given over to breakneck sprinting to Christmas morning.

Chasing Commercial Christmas

Our sprinting is often a ruse, the focus on countdown to Christmas, a diversion so we won't have to deal with the really deep parts of our lives, which seem to pop up with the tenacity of weeds in the cracks of the sidewalks of our carefully manicured personalities. Some parts take thought, reflection, and prayer. One teacher decided that she would try to break the chain of commercial Christmas, and for one year she did not participate in secret Santa and cookie exchanges of her school and with her friends. Instead she used the time and energy to find out more about herself and her longing to bring Christmas to children who really were hurting, children with their mothers in jail. She joined a group that gave books and tapes of the incarcerated parents reading the books to their children. She took a step toward finding a meaningful Christmas.

A Time of True Preparation

Historically in the church the four weeks before Christmas were a season of repentance to prepare our hearts to receive the gift of peace. The Pilgrims didn't tolerate festivity for the birth of Christ. The color of the altar paraments was somber purple just like those of the Lenten season. Many churches have moved to blue as the liturgical color for Advent, suggesting the purity of a young girl saying yes to God's invitation to share God's precious gift with humankind. But blue or purple, this time was set aside for waiting and watching. It was time to look at the weeds in our sidewalks and become attentive to what God could be doing in our lives. How does becoming attentive to what

God is doing in the world make me accountable for choices in my life? Have I lost my faith this year? Have I failed to acknowledge how my heart has been broken? For what am I grieving? What does all my hustle and bustle say about my trust in God?

It seems easier to fit one more thing into our schedule than to spend those twenty-eight days of Advent in quiet expectancy. We are fearful that if we looked more closely at December, we would find ourselves spiritually broken. People resist change fearing loss. And that they may awake like Scrooge on Christmas morning, wondering if they have missed it.

Looking in the Wrong Places

We fear TLC, "Too Little Currency." What would Christmas look like if we searched in the tradition of John the Baptist? Animal skins itch, and a diet of locust and wild honey would exacerbate our food allergies. Who needs that? But the truth of the matter is we fear we have too little currency to get a Christmas that can't be bought, ordered or delivered. John was getting us ready for a currency that reshaped our world. John, the wild man, said, "The real action comes next. The star in this drama, to whom I'm a mere stagehand, will change your life. I'm baptizing you here in the river, turning your old life in for a kingdom life. His baptism—a holy baptism by the Holy Spirit—will change you from the inside out" (*The Message*, Mark 1:7–8).

We fear that if we were changed from the inside out during this Advent, we wouldn't know ourselves. What parts of me that I value would have to go? What new attitudes and practices would I need to develop to overcome my fear of too little currency? Could I face the next two weeks of being poverty-stricken spiritually? The road is difficult, through scary deserts where we don't seem to have resources to get to that new understanding and perspective that we long for on sleepless nights. How would we manage without those crooked paths of our carefully constructed devices that keep us from finding God?

Empty Hands Receive Gifts

Those who have stayed the course and faced their apparent too little lack of currency have found such amazing things like their own calm presence even in the face of bare-bones existence that mimics the inner strengthening of winter's assault. Those who walk and work to make the rough places plain in their own lives have found a transparency that testifies quietly in deed and demeanor to a calmer Christmas.

As in traveling to another country, sometimes the currency we brought with us doesn't work in this new land. But there are Advent currency exchanges. The prophet Jeremiah noted, "The days are surely coming when the Lord will give us a heart to know the Lord; and we shall be God's people, God's alone, for we shall return to God with our whole heart (Jeremiah 7:24)." So we will not be afraid. Our fear of too little currency is exchanged for the currency of Christmas, which is the gift of a heart transplant.

Finding the New Currency

Here are two examples of those who have found delight and surprise as they found they had the currency to walk to Bethlehem. In a long line of waiting shoppers, a young mother told a harried shopper of her Christmas strategy for her young children. Each child received only three gifts. She reasoned very pragmatically. It was good enough for Mary's boy. It would be good enough for her children too. Frequent trips to the library were increasing her family's awareness of stories and the customs of Christmas around the world.

In the library of the Church of the Brethren in Lombard there is a wall of plaques with arks on the top of each award. Every year the small congregation raises five thousand dollars to fill an ark for Heifer International, which gives animals to families around the world to improve the quality of life and reduce infant mortality. The recipient families then pass on the blessing by giving the first offspring of their animal to another family. They give the revolving currency of abundance even in the midst of seeming scarcity.

Christmas through Different Eyes

John the Baptist was right. The one who baptizes with the Holy Spirit gives us a currency that is enough. Small gifts become manna. The currency of Christmas sensitizes our hearts to look beyond the immediacy of December 25 to walk the road where peace and righteousness kiss. Here God's justice pierces our hearts, and we discover that our currency, however small we believe it is, admits us to a banquet for all those who are cornered by life's difficult circumstances.

What will your Christmas morning be like? Life with a new heart? A glimpse of a path where human suffering is being addressed and reduced? A world headed toward righteousness? God's currency is sufficient. There is enough. Do we have the courage to live out of God's promise of new life? Lord Chesterton said it best. "It is not that Christianity has been tried and found wanting. It is that Christianity has never been tried." Imagine trading our anxiety and hectic pace for God's justice, a world where wolves and lambs dine together and the earth is full of the knowledge of God. We'd all want to spend Christmas and every day there. At God's currency exchange we can get Christmas hearts. There is enough for everyone. We have God's word on that. It is a promise upon which to spend our last dime. Amen.

Making Truffles

It started at a spring tea in a church basement. On a dainty plate there were truffles, chocolate inside and out with ribbons of white chocolate trailing across their tops. It has become an obsession—the pursuit of the perfect truffle. For as I was oohing and aahing about the dark smooth filling, my companion, Virginia, whispered a magic incantation in my ear. She had the truffle recipe. I was amazed that all that goodness could be found in only three ingredients. But ingredients are one thing. Making them into those gorgeous, mouth-watering bites was another. Thus began my journey into the land of truffles.

Three ingredients---one package of chocolate cookie sandwiches with white frosting centers, an eight-ounce package of cream cheese, and two cups of melting chocolate---have morphed into a foray of five years. The process has gotten better. What once took me several hours I have now streamlined to two, including chilling time. I used to end on my knees, carefully washing of the floor and looking for large globs and hidden smears of chocolate as my final act of obeisance to the chocolate gods, but I can now keep the cookie dust and chocolates smudges somewhat contained.

Beyond those three ingredients, Virginia sent two pages of directions for the neophyte. They didn't begin to cover the twists and turns on the road to truffledom. Rather the directions became stepping stones to discovery and the seeds of innovation in a sweet process. Truffles have become a metaphor of how to live.

I didn't think I could mess up mixing chocolate cookie sandwiches with cream cheese and then adding a chocolate coat. But as I discovered, there are necessary steps to ensure the perfect blending. You must separate the cookie from its white filling. I thought those cookies would just pull apart with a gentle twist and all the frosting would be on one side of the cookie. I was wrong, or maybe I just didn't have the knack. On good days I can twist the cookie sandwich apart and not break either half, but it is exceedingly rare that the frosting stays on one side, so I have to remove the frosting from both sides and put it in a bowl where the cream cheese awaits the frosting. The clean cookies then go in the food processor (in batches) to be ground to a fine powder. I learned this key step because too few twirls in the processor results in grainy candy and questioning glances from the truffle recipients that said, "Did you make these in the desert during a sandstorm?"

Mixing the cream cheese and frosting until the mixture is smooth is something I have down pat. Then the chocolate dust must be mixed into the frosting mixture (in batches) so the mixture becomes smooth. Next the goop must be dropped by rounded teaspoons on waxed paper on a tray and whisked into the freezer to thoroughly chill.

Here is where the real learning begins. What's happened up to this point is a honeymoon. The challenge awaits. The next part is like life. I have all the ingredients, and I am well into the process; however, the fine-tuning and repeated errors keep me aware that learning and imagining how to achieve new outcomes not only is key to creating a fabulous truffle but goes a long way in the game of life too.

When I first began making these truffles, I assembled drying racks with waxed paper beneath them. I gathered various spoons, forks, toothpicks, cups for melting the chocolate, and my instincts for cooking gathered from a lifetime of growing, cooking, and creating *home* with my food acumen. To begin the dipping process, I first took the pecan-sized globs of chilled filling and dropped them like bombs into the melted chocolate. Soon the filling and the coating were indistinguishable, as the heated chocolate and the cold filling created a lukewarm soup with soft lumps. Next batch I used a fork as a sling to launch the ball into the waiting chocolate. That was a mistake. By the time I coaxed the ball in melted chocolate and tried to retrieve it with a spoon, half of the melted chocolate was on one ball and rapidly dripping off the drying rack onto the waxed paper below. The upside was my husband got to eat a lot of "failed chocolate," but it was getting pricey when I was using a whole batch of melting chocolate for a few truffles that were as warty as toads in the aftermath.

Did I mention the temperature and consistency of the chocolate? I made huge progress in understanding how to melt the chocolate early on when I cranked up the microwave to a minute and a half and removed the cup to discover a holey, smelly mess at the bottom of the cup that tainted the entire batch. It was a short walk from the microwave to the garbage. Now I massage the chocolate with twenty-second zaps, relying on stirring to complete the melting process. It takes a whole lot of finesse here, like dealing with adolescent children, if I recall correctly.

Chocolate has its own temperament. I learned this by trying to introduce foreign substances like butter or milk to try to reach a softer consistency. They froze up like boiling water at the North Pole. Again there was the short walk from the microwave to the garbage. Learning chocolate's limits in a heated situation reflects my behavior in tense moments. Think about short walks to the garbage can.

We have a friend from Hungary who winters in Florida, and although she understands English perfectly, she is reticent to jump into the English-speaking pool and start swimming. Mary did want to learn to make truffles. We both thought cooking together would be a great way for us to communicate better since I speak no Hungarian. Well, it was hard to tell who the teacher was and who the student was as Mary was an ophthalmologist with an engineer's brain for imagining structural changes. By this time my truffle-making was in its toothpick phase, and I would spear a hardened ball of candy, rotate it in the melted chocolate, and quickly bring it to the drying rack. The dismounting trick required one to slide the toothpick out against the edge of the rack, resulting in severely misshapen and disfigured truffles, some with broken toothpicks inside.

Mary endured my ineptness, and when she went home to make them herself, she simply used a drying rack with feet that raised the rack a few inches above the counter. (Don't tell Mary, but I had one in my baking cabinet.) When I tried her innovation, I was amazed at how quick and easy it was to disengage the truffle from the toothpick by simply thrusting the toothpick gently through any hole on the drying rack. Gentle motion is important, for the next step is to chill the truffle and then remove it from the rack without leaving globs of hardened chocolate and filling stuck to the drying rack.

We are always adapting and changing, and now I have learned the wisdom of small batches. I now only take a few chilled globs out of the freezer at a time. This keeps the filling hard, and it can more quickly receive the chocolate. I roll the filling in my hands to make a rounder ball before its chocolate plunge. It is getting a more truffly shape.

The saga continues. This year the problem of the sticking hardened chocolate on the racks will be addressed. I'm considering a candle to soften the edges. (Don't you love the romantic imagery?)

I will continue to put each truffle in one of those tiny cupcake papers. They make each truffle seem like a special gift. I don't know if this Christmas I will finally nail truffle-making, but the hours I have spent in its pursuit have taught me valuable lessons. I may never get it right, but the fact that I am willing to try is pleasing to the truffle gods. There are others on the same journey, and they may have greater skills and insights than I have. I can learn by walking with them.

My husband and I don't eat a lot of truffles. We give them away as gifts, a few at a time. Arranged six or seven blossoming on a festive dessert plate with each truffle making another petal, they resemble daisies. There is a deep joy in hoping that someone will feel in those tiny morsels the goodness and love the Truffle Maker has for each of us.

Human Rights Day

Today is Human Rights Day. Back on December 10, 1948 the newly formed United Nations adopted the Universal Declaration of Human Rights. It was conceived as a "common standard of achievement for all people and all nations" with the hopes of becoming a yardstick by which to measure ourselves in the pursuit of raising the world's people into the community where persons are valued, cherished, and can thrive as individuals and as community, country, and world citizens. Reading the thirty principles of the declaration covers the waterfront of rights and responsibilities for creating a healthy fabric of society.

Looking with thanks on our Advent calendars, we are grateful for reminders that we are walking our journeys to help all men and women realize they are brothers and sisters and children of the Creator, who wants us to live in harmony.

What goes around comes around. This time it is more than twenty-six centuries later as we read the words of the prophet Isaiah. He wrote as Judah was in crisis, and Isaiah passionately shares his vision of human rights for God's beloved people.

The wolf will live with the lamb,

the leopard will lie down with the goat,

the calf and the lion and the yearling together;

and a little child will lead them.

The cow will feed with the bear,

their young will lie down together,

and the lion will eat straw like the ox.

The infant will play near the hole of the cobra,

and the infant child put his hand into the viper's nest.

They will neither hurt nor destroy on all my holy mountain,

for the earth will be full of the knowledge of the Lord

as the waters cover the earth (Isaiah 11:6–9 New International Version).

Holiday Traffic

When I was a little girl growing up on a farm in the rolling hills of the Finger Lakes of New York state, holiday traffic meant there might be a lot of folks traveling on state routes 5 and 20, which were the two-and three-lane highways we took to visit our aunts and uncles for Thanksgiving, Christmas, and Easter family dinners. We didn't travel great distances, yet we anticipated those dinners with great enthusiasm. I must have been about ten when my father bought a new Ford, and the family would pile into the car for the thirty-five-mile drive in one direction to visit one set of cousins or the interminable ride to visit our cousins who lived forty miles in the other direction. That trip included many traffic lights. It seemed to my impatient soul trapped between older siblings in the back seat just short of eternity. Those hours were some of the longest of my childhood.

As fond as these memories were, I was more than willing to join travelers who took to the friendly skies as air travel gave new meaning to my childhood notions of holiday traffic. It was all so sophisticated and glamorous when I took my first plane trip to Boston to go to another family gathering, this time to visit my boyfriend's family. And it lived up to expectations except for spilling coffee on my white pleated skirt, and I disembarked a little less together than I had envisioned in my mind's eye.

Yet traveling to visit family for the holidays maintains its magic for me, even though now I am a grandmother of six and my two children and their families live hundreds of miles away from home. The thought of seeing the children and hearing all the cute and funny things children do captures my imagination even before we go online to get our tickets. Home for the holidays means I am going to be with the children. Let the games begin. Home is those precious faces who create the better world of magic and possibility. That's where I live. So this Christmas I didn't mind a bit when we had to roll out of bed at four in the morning, even though we had gotten home from Christmas Eve services just a few hours earlier. We were joining the parade of pilgrims going home for the holidays. Home is where the heart is.

I was a little concerned when the taxi service my husband had been using didn't show up at five thirty for our 7:25 a.m. flight. This one-man taxi service had stopped by our house and asked my normally intelligent husband to pay for the ride a week in advance. My kind and generous husband had included a twenty-dollar tip in his prepayment. My prompt and thorough husband was now frantically punching numbers on the phone, and he finally made contact with a slurred voice explaining he was at the hospital and couldn't make the run today.

More punched numbers and a miracle occurred. My husband, through the force of his fingertips, reached another company who promised to get us to the airport in time to catch our flight. Our driver must have had NASCAR training, for he perfected the rolling stop and the accelerated yellow-light maneuver several times in the fourteen-mile trip to the airport. Flying through the lines, we were imagining our high fives as we settled into our assigned seats. Nobody traveled on Christmas Day. We crashed to reality when we hit the queue for inspection of our personal items. We hadn't anticipated the couple with three kids carrying their personal effects for a Mount Everest ascent directly ahead of us.

Leaping and dashing, we headed for the gate only to find the gate area packed with folks who had apparently made better ground transportation than we had. Panting heavily, my frequent-flyer husband put on his soothing and supportive voice to ask the harried gate agent the reason why all these folks were milling around like cattle at the defunct Chicago Stockyards. Equally patient and soothing, the gate agent counseled, "Just listen for my announcement."

"Ladies and gentlemen, the captain has just informed me that the plane will have to be de-iced before takeoff. We hope to be ready to board the plane in forty-five minutes. Perhaps you would like to get some breakfast before boarding." The rest of his message was lost in our loud breathing as we tried to get our heart rates and blood pressure low enough to be considered safe for boarding." Three hours and no breakfast later, a full flight of sullen passengers boarded an airplane that had been de-iced twice because the sprayer had broken just shy of completion the first time. Our traveling companions' tropical shirts could no longer camouflage their irritation that they had missed their connecting flight to a tropical paradise. They would have to see the gate agent when they disembarked the plane. For us it was just a tweak and not a new game plan.

Tumbling and shoving out of the plane, we resembled lemmings heading for the White Cliffs of Dover. The agents booked on us a connecting flight. Fortunately a three-hour delay couldn't squelch our joy. Unfortunately that three-hour delay plus the fact that the flight to Ft. Lauderdale had been canceled because of the heavy holiday traffic meant that we would now be flying to Miami. There we were told we could take a bus back to Ft. Lauderdale Airport to get a taxi to Christmas. This three-hour wait for our connecting flight plus the bus and taxi rides meant we would miss our granddaughters' delight as they opened their gifts. Three- and five-year-olds can wait just so long to see the holiday unfold. To console ourselves we ate voraciously in the grazing area of the airline club lounge. This time we boarded the plane with openly sullen and quiet folks who barely spoke as they shuffled to their seats. Apparently their planes had also been delayed because of de-icing.

Arriving in sunny Miami, which was cloudy, windy, and overcast, we gathered our luggage and made a beeline for the airport bus stand only to find out they had closed at 5:00 p.m. so that their employees could celebrate with their families. Now I am all for family celebrations on the holidays. Meanwhile my logical and methodical husband began to hail limo drivers until he found one that would drive us to Ft. Lauderdale Airport. He already had two other passengers. It seemed holiday traffic could either defeat us or strengthen our resolve. With the grace of hurdle jumpers, we climbed over the woman who had picked up some of the bags of the mountain climbers and the quiet, compact gentleman who neither looked at nor spoke to us.

When those two were free of the limo, my savvy husband moved toward the driver's window and queried if he could take us to Christmas instead of the airport. He didn't think it was a good idea but agreed to do it just as the interstate signs indicated he would have to make the choice between the airport and Christmas. He then called to my husband, who was smiling broadly, thinking we were home free. The driver began, "Sir, the engine is dying. It wouldn't be a good idea if I had a breakdown and was going away from the airport." He pulled into the right lane, and the noise from his engine got louder. We moved slower and slower until our magic carpet died on the turn into the airport.

Believe it or not, there was not a lot of traffic. The three of us sat there while the driver called his dispatcher, who couldn't promise any help because everyone had the day off. Bravely he stood outside his limo and finally hailed a cab who would take us and our luggage to Christmas. My compassionate and big-hearted husband gave the driver a generous tip, and we boarded yet another conveyance for our trip to Christmas.

I was tired, disheveled, disappointed, and out of sorts when my husband leaned over and whispered in my ear, "Mary, this is Joseph. Are we there yet?"

Christmas calls for housekeeping. Homes cleaned, windows sparkling and our hearts clean to be truly ready.

The Forgiveness Piece

Rembrandt's masterpiece *The Return of the Prodigal Son* resides now in Russia's amazing art museum, the Hermitage, in St. Petersburg. The scene is based on Jesus' story of the father and his two sons told in Luke 15. I became curious about what Rembrandt had captured in the painting as I read Henri Nouwen's book, *The Return of the Prodigal Son*. I persuaded my husband that we needed to see it for ourselves, so off we went to Russia. Inside the gallery he tipped a guide, and I got to spend ten or fifteen minutes alone with this great painting. It is massive, dark, and illuminating simultaneously. Rembrandt placed the characters on his canvas to evoke the various roles we play throughout our lifetime in Jesus' story of longing and forgiving. Using two planes and his golden light, he captured the complexity of this spiritual task.

Rembrandt uses a diagonal plane from the upper left corner to the lower right. A woman is almost hidden in the shadowy upper left corner. In dark shadows openness and curiosity are revealed on her face. Continuing forward on that diagonal plane, there is an older woman. Her gray head has wide eyes, and her face is softened by her unfailing gaze on the supplicant. I can see a peace filling in the wrinkles of long-carried worry. The third character on this diagonal plane is a seated man. He is much more clearly visible in the foreground. He is a witness to the emotional event but not a participant in it. While one hand holds his shawl, a disproportionately big hand holds his crossed leg. His equally big foot suggests ambivalence between staying and leaving, and he has steeled himself to stay. This diagonal plane extends from left background to right foreground, continuing out toward the viewer. Everything on this plane is shadowy, made even darker by contrast with the golden light of the second plane.

We are witnesses to this homecoming on the central plane of the painting. Three figures dominate, but the golden light falls most directly on the old man's serene face. His brilliant crimson robe covers his shoulders, both stooped and yet powerful through his journey of disappointment, suffering, longing, and hope. The old man's hands rest in blessing on the back of his son, who has knelt before his father. While the father's arms wear many bracelets denoting wealth, it is his hands that draw attention. The right hand, which is smoother with tapered fingers, is reminiscent of a woman's hand, while the left hand is thicker with stubby fingers like a man's.

The son's cloak is tattered. The prodigal has come home with one sandal flopping and the other without a sole, expecting to receive his father's wrath. The light of heaven shines upon the father, who had such longing, and the son, who had such need. The son's hair is matted to his head, suggesting the head of a baby emerging from the birth canal. Father stoops to his son; the son leans toward his father.

There is a second less illuminated crimson cape. It rests on the older brother's shoulders as he watches the scene unfold in front of him. Leaning heavily on his walking stick, disdain pours out of his every pore. He hoped he would never see this reconciliation.

My foot swings back and forth in the pew. Pastor Sam is talking about forgiveness in this sermon. Peter asked Jesus how many times he has to forgive. I swing my foot more vigorously, trying to distract myself from the words that I really need to hear. "Forgiveness," Pastor Sam says, "is only possible with God's grace, and for grace to be available, it is necessary to get in a right relationship with God." The older brother's piety is the accumulation of all duties, tasks, and good deeds laboriously and joylessly performed for an altogether unworthy class of miscreants. He has fulfilled the duties of a dutiful older brother while "that son of yours," he tells his father, has wandered down paths of dissolute living and faddish salvations.

Pastor Sam continues, "It's difficult to get to the grace of God because you have to first become humble before God." I imagine the older brother whipping from his girdle a complete and annotated list of all the things he has done for the father, all the ways he has covered for the derelict, and an equally long list of those who never bothered to express thanks for his Herculean effort on behalf of the family. And while he was out in the field and managing the family farm, his father has gone gaga over the ne'er-do-well. "It is our own need to be forgiven that keeps us from forgiving others," Sam says. "It's knowing that you have been forgiven that makes it possible to start forgiving yourself." By now my foot is swinging in wide circles at breakneck speed. Like the older son I ask why I need to be forgiven. I have spent a lifetime fulfilling what was expected of a dutiful daughter, a supporting wife, and a nurturing mother. My circling foot reveals I am still caught in the snare of the unforgiven. Why do I need this forgiveness? Is it for my generosity, my diligence, my ability to complete tough tasks? I sense the older brother is sitting right beside me in the pew.

The pastor probes on like a doctor looking for the cyst that is causing so much pressure on its host. "You must let go of your need to be right," Sam suggests. The thought doesn't thrill me. I have a very refined sense of good taste, and I am assured in my theology, opinions, and beliefs. If it's not broken, why fix it? "Clinging to our need to be right or our scantily clothed greed, power, or self-congratulatory 'I told you so' attitude is merely another layer of fat, an insulation from being hurt again, and God knows we have been hurt so many times," he says, summarizing my case.

"Hurt people hurt people," the pastor says, but then he alludes to other skills and feelings we also carry within us that can grow and nurture us when the urgent need for forgiveness comes to the front and center in our lives. God's grace comes unexpectedly like rain in the desert. Some can cup their hands in supplication so that they can receive the quenching water for their souls. Right now the gift of listening to the howling winds of the desert, to Simon and Garfunkel's *Sound of Silence*, or to the endless crashing of the waves on the beach is where I need to focus. Listen to what others are saying and conversely what they are not saying. Try to imagine how they might have arrived where they are now. What voices, silences, and shadowy images have shaped our relentless enemies? What sins of the fathers visited them?

Forgiveness seems an insurmountable climb. It reminds me of other hurts. I fear that my anger and pain might be publically addressed. Try as I may to control them, to keep them tucked away, those whom I dislike, my prodigals, often arrive unbidden as grief. It will require unimagined courage to look at a tormentor and see who it really is. In seeing the object of my scorn, I will see my own face, the part that would love to do just what "that son of yours" has done. Pogo, the cartoon character, reminds us that we have met the enemy and he is us. Is Rembrandt inviting the older brother within each of us to drop our self-righteous attitudes and kneel before the welcoming father?

Pastor Sam leans into the pulpit and gives us his parting shot. "Pray," he intones, "for those who have hurt you. Your faltering prayers for those who have hurt you beyond your endurance are your doorway to freedom."

I think about Rembrandt's masterpiece. The father's hands rest upon the prodigal. The other son straightened his back. As he walked from the room of reconciliation, there is an air of anticipation for the feast, laughter and soul-satisfying aromas of the fatted calf on the spit. But the figures are on two planes in this painting. It is the father who first calls the prodigal "this son of mine." He willingly received his wayward son. We can follow the drama of the story as our eyes travel around the painting. Our eyes first travel to the other brother, and we see the hardness in his eyes as our eyes follow his to the golden embrace of father and son. Even the floor where they stand is swathed in golden light, so different from the floor where the older son stands. Our eyes are then swept back to the three figures on the diagonal plane.

Rembrandt's interpretation and light shows us how we are all players in the drama. It is hopeful. God's grace comes as we understand that we are all participants in the eternal drama. We are the watchers peering to see how the golden light falls and heals. We watch, sometimes with dispassion, sometimes with longing. We also may step into the golden light. We are offered the starring roles. Will we acknowledge our brokenness and need for healing relationships? Will we stand back in judgment and loneliness, or will we be the one to open our arms in embrace? Faltering prayer, seeing ourselves as prodigals, acknowledging our hardness and disease become occasions of that breaking light. Spiritual housekeeping makes room for more light and truth into the dark nights of our souls. Rembrandt holds all these roles in tension in *The Return of the Prodigal Son*. He invites us into the immensity of grace and the freedom and joy of healed relationships. Pastor Sam is right. Our wobbly steps toward God offer our best shot to healthy hearts and shining windows of our souls this Christmas.

St. Lucia Day

Lucia was a young girl of Syracuse, Sicily, who lived during the persecution of the Roman emperor Diocletian. The legend of Lucy, like many martyrs of the early fourth century, was that she was the daughter of wealthy parents. Her father died when she was a child. Lucia consecrated her life to God and her dowry to the poor, but this news incensed her fiancé, who appealed to the governor of Syracuse. The governor commanded her to sacrifice to the emperor's image. She refused, was tortured, and died in 304 CE.

Lucia, whose name comes from the Latin word *lux,* which means light, became identified with the winter solstice, where her light would brighten a dark, winter world. St. Lucia Day is particularly celebrated in the Scandinavian countries. In the eighteenth century Lucia was first celebrated in Sweden in a winter festival. Today the oldest daughter in the family wears a white robe with a wreath of candles on her head. Before dawn St. Lucia brings buns and coffee to her family. In Stockholm there is a huge celebration in the city center on the night of December 13. Receiving Lucia's light will enable everyone to endure the winter darkness.

St. Lucia Buns

3/4 cup milk scalded	1/4 cup butter or margarine
1/2 cup warm water	4 to 5 cups flour
1 t. salt	1/2 t. saffron threads
2 packages dry yeast	1 T. boiling water
1/2 cup sugar	plump raisins
1 beaten egg	

Add salt, sugar, and butter to scalded milk. Cool. Soak saffron in boiling water. Cool. Measure a half cup of water into a large mixing bowl. Sprinkle in yeast, stirring until dissolved. Add milk and saffron mixtures and two cups of flour. Beat until smooth. Add enough flour to make a thick dough that can be kneaded on a lightly floured board until smooth and elastic, which takes about eight minutes.

Place in a greased bowl, turning ball of dough to coat completely. Cover with plastic wrap and then a dish towel, and let rise in a warm place until doubled in bulk. Punch down, cut into eighteen equal strips, and roll each into a twelve-inch rope. Start at one end and roll into a coil, stopping at the center. Then roll in the reverse direction from the other end of the strip to make an S-shaped coil. Place on a lightly buttered baking sheet, cover, and let rise another thirty minutes.

Just before baking in a preheated 350-degree oven, put a raisin deep in the center of both ends of each coil. Bake for fifteen minutes. Brush the top lightly with salted butter. Cool on wire racks.

Lucia's Light

Tell the tale of simple maiden living centuries ago,
Carried love and God's compassion, serving those by power bent low.
Many ages have now vanished, still we see Lucia's spark,
Offering solace to those suffering, giving courage in the dark.

Maiden from the isle of Sicily, she still stands erect and tall.
God was speaking through that maiden—mighty voice from one so small.
Roman emperors, local governors watched amazed at Lucia's truth
Bringing hope to those who suffer, bringing hope despite her youth.

Silenced, martyred by the empire, in time Lucia's story spread
To those dark lands' barren winter, to those hungry for hope's bread.
In the midst of deep oppression, still her light reveals the dawn
Born in mangers, born in ghettoes, hope of ages, Christmas morn.

If the light of simple maiden traveling 'cross the wintry world
Brings the hope of God's rich promise, how much more can we observe?
Eat her golden bread rejoicing, bear her light to darkest sites,
Herald God's surprising victory—Jesus' birth puts fear to flight.

Copyright Elaine Eachus, 2012 Hymn Tune: "Scarlet Ribbons"

Edward and the Language of Love

I was recovering from cancer. The second surgery had been successful. Radiation was over, but deep wounds on my spirit remained. Even the lilac bush blooming at the side door did little to move me into joy of an ebullient Illinois spring. A couple in our bridge group had mentioned that they had two litters of kittens. They had bought a horse farm about an hour away. On a whim I called to see if I could come and look at the kittens. It was there where I lost my heart. He and his three sisters were curled up with their mother in a barn. He was the standout. His sisters were spitting images of their tiger-gray-striped mother, but this one was special. When our friends bought the farm, they inherited a wild chocolate point Siamese cat with it. They had never caught him, but he apparently caught the eye of lots of the female barn cats, for some kittens bore resemblance to the feral king of the ranch.

Our little guy was totally creamy white. His ears and his tail bore telltale traces that would become darker over time. His tail would be marked with a few raccoon rings in honor of his mother; the rest of him was a tribute to his father's strong genes. He was probably five weeks old at the time, and I should have left him longer with his family. But I had such a strong need to focus on something other than my illness that I asked if I could bring him home that day. With two litters of kittens and probably more on the way, there was little resistance to my plan. The pint-sized passenger rode home in silence in the back seat of my Honda.

We named him Edward for Edward Scissorhands, for his nails were as sharp as scissors, we discovered, and he wasn't particularly proficient in withdrawing them from our flesh. I needed that one-man show moving about our house. His antics delighted us. He bumped into more than the average corners because his eyes were crossed. He loved to chase reflected spots of light on the wall. He was a perfect cat for me. However, he only had eyes for my husband. He was oblivious to the fact that it was I who fed him, gave him fresh water, and kept his box pristine. It was my husband, Ace, whom he adored.

Now Edward was not given to overt displays of affection. He soon made it clear that affection would be dispensed on Edward's timetable and at Edward's initiation. Also Edward would not be picked up under any circumstances. That was beneath his Siamese dignity. There would be no petting of anything but his head and shoulders; scratching ears or stroking tummies were manners for cats of lesser breeding. To make sure these rules were enforced, Edward would turn and face away from you if he was going to let you give him affection at all. It took him quite a while to train us; however, in his adolescence he discovered his hiss, and we were eventually trained. We found our routine. I fed, watered, and cleaned. Edward rewarded Ace with appropriate affection as he deemed necessary, but always he faced away so he could beat a hasty retreat when he overdosed on affection. As the years went by, usually at night he would sometimes jump into my husband's chair, face the front, and settle in on Ace's lap.

Grandchildren began arriving. This was a difficult adjustment for Edward. He would hiss and spit and lacked the good sense to just run away. His territorial imperative was invaded; he felt impelled to defend his turf. One set of grandchildren feared him, refusing to come in the house until we put Edward outside. The other set found him funny or generally ignored him.

When we started spending the winters in Florida, Edward began logging frequent flyer miles. He always did that under a dose of tranquilizers, but he loved lying in the Florida sun streaming in our windows in the morning. Afternoons were devoted to sleeping in his wingback chair. When we went out of the house, Edward would position himself on the living room floor so he could see if anyone came in the front or kitchen door. Here he would sleep with the characteristic Siamese pose of one forepaw extended and the other curled beneath him.

One of the things we miss most about Edward is that there is no one waiting for us when we come home. But I don't want you to think that we haven't learned the lessons Edward came to teach us. We have. We are most grateful.

One of our grandchildren is language-delayed, and as his years increase, so does his frustration. Yet having lived for almost eighteen years with Edward, we learned that while others may not meet expectations for how relationships would play out, there is still joy to be shared. When you learn the rules for another's well-being, there are the loveliest surprises in your new role. The ability to imagine another's experience softens you to see, as post-moderns know, that truth is seldom spelled with a capital T. Every once in a while you are able to glimpse yourself as Jesus hoped when he told us, "Unless you become as a child—"

That time for me was last summer when Ace and I were spending the day at Navy Pier in Chicago with our daughter-in-law and grandchildren. The day was a kaleidoscope of images—children riding the speedboat, seeing the city rise at our feet on the Ferris wheel, watching our bodies distort in the wall of mirrors. We did a huge amount of walking, and our grandson was enjoying the day; however, it was noisy and crowded. It was a cacophony of sensory intake, and his anxiety was increasing. We were headed for yet another adventure in the late afternoon when unannounced and unexpectedly my grandson started to walk beside me and took my hand. Unbidden, he had chosen me as his companion for a few minutes—his terms, his time. My heart filled with unexpected joy. I thought of Edward and how he taught us the language of love.

TLC: The Long-Distance Call

A Sermon for the Third Sunday in Advent

Techno-Christmas

Your new smart phone is well on its way to obsolescence. You need to pay close attention to the parades of apps and technological innovations of newer phones, TVs, and cameras. Long-distance phone calls are as archaic as stegosaurus and saber-toothed tigers when in a few keystrokes you can communicate virtually any place Verizon or T-Mobile have service. Your children will scratch their heads in wonder when you to refer to Grandma's long-distance call or wonder why you could only call home from college on Sundays when the phone rates were lower. Being "with it" is a highly prized quality both in life and in technology. To remain on top of this techno heap, it is good to access someone under twenty. Yet as unlikely as it may seem, we may be listening for a long-distance call.

Something's Missing

The long-distance call (TLC) comes from unlikely places. It is a niggling feeling deep within. Like a line of a song that runs through our minds but one to which we can't quite recall the entirety of lyrics, it camps on the doorstep of our hearts, seeking attention. Blues artists and psalmists have the knack for getting our attention through a phrase or a soulful line. They evoke the memory of those moments, which we have carefully packed away but which, when we least expect them, pop out like unwanted stepchildren with dirty feet. But we do listen for that call in December. We'd like to hear the voice reminding us of the world transformed. Remind us again of that soul-healing laughter spilling from children laughing and playing in the streets of Chicago, Damascus, or Ramallah. Our careful responses and proper planning are designed to keep away the pain of the brokenness in the world and brokenness we feel within ourselves, places where alienation, suffering, and feelings of abandonment huddle together. Hatred and shutting our feelings off have been easier strategies than standing before God and acknowledging what we are feeling. It's easier to keep up the charade than to face the littered battleground of our losses and grief.

That Haunting Call

But there is something about preparing for Christmas that loosens those feelings that have been packed away like our Christmas decorations. Prophets of old carried the laments and the corporate sins of the people in order to bring them to the forefront and to keep them before the people until they could hear calls for repentance from the One who takes tears and grief and grows them into justice and joy. We long for that call but fear it will mean further struggle. We reason it might be better to turn off the phone than deal with all the intractable problems with which we have been able to do nothing.

Nevertheless, Advent is that time when we stop in midstep between the post office and Macy's and wonder what God is doing. What is God passionate about, and what could God's purpose be in this fast-paced confusion where we find ourselves? Could God really answer our deep longing? Psalm 146 tells us the happy ones are those who rely on God and see how God is executing justice for all those forgotten. Really? Seriously? Could this time bring us to where there is good news for the brokenhearted, where those in captivity to all sorts of addictions, denials, and oppression could find redemption? Would looking out over the world and our lives as God does bring us to a place of comfort, the release of prisoners in jail and prisoners incarcerated in their own devices? Do we really have to look amid the pain and the ruins? Why do those voices of the hurting world clamor for our time and attention right smack dab in the middle of our countdown to Christmas? Mary answered God's call and believed her saying yes to God would indeed scatter the proud, bring down those who lorded their power over others, and send the rich away empty-handed. Grateful Mary praises God.

Voices from Afar

Paul Simon, poet and songwriter, sensed the tension between what is and what we most need in his Grammy-winning album, *Graceland*. In the first track "The Boy in the Bubble," he writes:

> These are the days of miracle and wonder
>
> This is the long distance call
>
> The way the camera follows us in slo-mo
>
> The way we look to us all
>
> The way we look to a distant constellation
>
> That's dying in a corner of the sky
>
> These are the days of miracle and wonder
>
> And don't cry baby, don't cry.

For miracle and wonder, there is a part of us that cries. Amid our busyness we are still haunted by the agonies of racism, religious bigotry, and violence gone mad. Tim DeChristopher was concerned about our dying planet when he fought to save Utah's wilderness lands from the sale of drilling rights. At the auction of those rights in December 2008 he picked up a paddle and began bidding on the leases as "Bidder 70." He won $1.8 million worth of parcels and inflated the price of many others. When it was discovered that he had no money to back his bids, the auction had to be shut down.

Tim DeChristopher was sentenced to two years in prison, but his boldness stopped the sale of twenty-two thousand acres of scenic wilderness. He said, "I thought I was sacrificing my freedom, but instead I was grabbing onto my freedom and refusing to let go of it for the first time" (*Yes!* Magazine, Summer 2013, Issue 66, p.23–24). The Bureau of Land Management had to scrap a rescheduled auction because it had skimped on its environmental analysis and inadequately consulted with the National Park Service. In 2013 a federal court denied an energy industry appeal to reinstate the leases.

Making Connections

If you are going to tell the story of God, you will also tell the story of the people. If you are telling the story of the people, then you will also tell the story of God. We fear that long-distance call because God is holding the mirror up for us to see ourselves as the actors and participants in God's story. Jim Wallis in his new book, *On God's Side: What Religion Forgets and Politics Hasn't Learned about Serving the Common Good,* tells of a United Methodist church in a suburb of Memphis, Tennessee. Heartsong Church responded to the announcement an Islamic cultural center was moving into their neighborhood with a big sign: "Welcome Memphis Islamic Center." The Muslims paid the pastor a visit, inquiring about the sign, and he told them about Jesus' command for welcoming neighbors. Soon there were barbecues serving halal meat, Christian and Muslim kids playing together, and adults tutoring inner-city kids and feeding the homeless together.

Pastor Stone actually got a long-distance call from Pakistan, a region where the United States has concentrated its drone strikes, from a group of Muslim men who had seen a segment on CNN about the Memphis welcome. A voice said to Stone, "I think God may be speaking to us through (you)." Another said through the help of an interpreter, "He went up to a little church near our mosque and he cleaned it, inside and out, scrubbed it." Another said, "We called to tell you, Pastor, tell your congregation we don't hate you. We love you. And because of what you did, we're going to take care of that little church."

Listen!

It's up to us! To answer the long-distance call is sure to bring dislocation of some plans for Christmas. But imagine the joy and connection when this call is not just one more thing to do on our to-do lists. It will be like that highway in Isaiah 35 where the redeemed return to God, singing and rejoicing. It is our opportunity to reconnect with God by being present with others.

Remember the encounter of Mary with her older cousin, Elizabeth, when they were both pregnant. Elizabeth intuited that her cousin was pregnant with the divine child. Leaving our to-do lists and projects, we can hear voices of prophets and angels calling us. So as we move closer to Christmas, listen for the long-distance call. Those who actually pay attention to those far-out and faraway voices envision a new reality. In answering the long-distance call, we become God's people, longing and looking for God's justice right here right now. We will together reach Bethlehem in time for an amazing birth of our humanity. Amen.

Christmas Cookies

Lucille reached for the refrigerator door with little enthusiasm but seriously hoped for a surprise. She hadn't planned on being here for Christmas, but her usually organized demeanor had crumbled in the past week. Trying to close up the condo as well as get things marked and sorted had taken her far longer than her organized mind could have imagined. She earned her livelihood, and her reputation was well-known in Syracuse, where her left brain had brought order to corporate chaos and poor management practices. Her keen eye had helped several companies see where new practices could carve out a future while their competitors were liquidating assets and trying to stay afloat.

Spending the week before Christmas in Ft. Lauderdale was a stroke of genius. After all, getting out of the frigid cold the week before Christmas could have some extremely positive side effects, like leaving her heavy scarves, boots, and parka in the closet and putting a pair of shorts, a bathing suit, her running shoes, and pairs of sandals in her carry-on bag. There was very little business activity the week before Christmas anyway. She imagined dining on Las Olas and enjoying a walk on the beach when sorting, stacking, and organizing became tedious. Lucille was glad things had worked out so positively. Her father, who had been a widower since her mother had died when Lucille was twenty-two, had asked her to close his condo on the beach. After all these years he had married a vivacious widow, and they had moved to Tucson. Lucille was delighted to do this for her father, for he had been her closest friend. This would be one Christmas gift she would gladly give.

"Close up the condo, take what you and Bruce might want, send the pictures and whatever things I might need, and get rid of the rest. That would be a huge gift for Jeannine and me. The realtor will be taking care of the closing the first week in January," her father had instructed.

Her eye was drawn to an old photograph she hadn't yet removed from the fridge. She and Bruce were spending a long weekend here with her father. How happy the three of them looked! She smiled. Now Bruce traveled extensively, making it home for about two weeks out of the month. Sometimes Lucille could join Bruce in another country, and she was always enthralled by the sights and sounds of the world, while at home she was building her reputation on her incisive ability to cut through the extraneous and get to the heart of the matter.

Lucille was surprised by how long it was taking her to decide what to do with the things of the life she and her parents had once shared. Removing the magnet, she took the photograph and put it in the pile marked Syracuse. She heard the door slam closed on the condo across the hall. She knew that meant that the nine-year-old son of the single mom had come home from school. It was two thirty, and she hadn't eaten lunch.

When she returned to the refrigerator, she opened the door to no surprise. There were the three yogurts and a mystery box she had brought home from restaurant dining. She only had today and tomorrow to get everything organized, boxed, and labeled for the movers. The day after tomorrow was Christmas, and she was going home.

Lucille decided against the refrigerator menu, put on her running shoes, and was heading for the convenience store when the nine-year-old dashed out his door across the hall and headed for the elevator. His wiry frame was a bundle of energy as he pushed the elevator button impatiently. With a skateboard under his arm, he kept fidgeting, waiting for the elevator to arrive. They rode in silence to the ground floor. She saw his shoulders slump perceptibly when his quick glance revealed none of his buddies were there to play. Clearly he was planning to spend some quality time in the skate park.

"Darn it," Alex muttered under his breath. "They couldn't escape."

"Your friends couldn't make it?" Lucille queried.

"Yep. Must have a lot of homework, and sometimes Juan has to help take care of his little sister."

"Bummer," Lucille sympathized. "I can tell that skateboard needs a workout." For the first time Alex looked up at the tall redhead and was greeted by her bemused smile. She remembered her disappointment when her friends couldn't play when she was his age.

"Hey, I've got an idea," she continued. "I am going to the mini-mart to get something for lunch. It's only a couple of blocks. You want to skate, and I could try to keep up with you. We could call your mom and let her know where we are going."

Alex sized her up. He had no friends to skate with. Well, maybe he could get a Gatorade out of the deal. "Sure, but I'll have to let my mom know." Lucille reached for her cell phone, and when Alex explained to his mother, she had no objections. She remembered Lucille's father fondly, for he had always been kind to her and Alex.

At the convenience store Alex got Gatorade and ranch dressing Doritos. Lucille abandoned her plan of a granola bar and fruit for Doritos too. Taking her change, they settled at one of the two bistro tables in front of the store. "You're good on that board," Lucille began. "I was running at a pretty good clip to keep up with you."

"You were really good," Alex conceded. "Do you run a lot?"

"I used to in high school, and I still like to run on the beach. I bet you really like sports, don't you?" Lucille noted the tanned leg swaying like a pendulum under the table.

"Yeah, my mom calls me 'Gone with the Wind.' I can beat most of the kids in my class. I usually get picked first for baseball because I can run the bases so fast."

"Maybe tomorrow we can run a little on the beach. Ask your mom, Alex. The next day I am going home."

"But it's Christmas."

Lucille finished the contents of the dresser in the bedroom. Most of the clothes she marked for the Goodwill box. She was surprised how long she took going through her mother's jewelry. It was just costume jewelry, but she touched the pins, remembering how her mother always wore a pin on her dress and how late in her life she had gotten her ears pierced. Lucille picked up the silver earrings she had gotten her mother for a birthday right after her mother had gotten sick. They looked like silver wings, small with finely sculpted lines that resembled feathers. She pulled off the backing and put them in her own earlobes. "I can't believe how long this is taking me. Down here I seem to have lost my touch. Thank goodness I am not like this in Syracuse. I'd be out of a job," she mused.

The next day Lucille tackled the kitchen. She flew through the cabinets, and the boxes stacked for Goodwill grew throughout the morning. She pitched the shelf paper from the cabinets, and soon even the garbage can was bulging. As she reached the kitchen junk drawer, she quickly dispensed with bits of tape and ribbon, odd screws, tiny packets with a few sheets of post-its left on them. It was about noon when she reached the bottom of the junk drawer, and there she found a stained and forgotten recipe card. She looked at the familiar, perfectly formed letters of her mother's Zaner-Bloser penmanship and read about the butter, flour, confectioner's sugar, lemon juice, zest, and eggs. *This is crazy*, she thought.

Nevertheless, Lucille tied on her running shoes, grabbed a twenty, and headed for the convenience store. A half an hour later Lucille was tearing open taped boxes marked for Goodwill, looking for a mixing bowl, juicer, and a square baking pan. By one thirty the condo was filled with the tangy smell of lemon, and by two thirty when she heard the door slam on the condo across the hall, the powdery confectioner's sugar had covered the top of her eight-by-eight-inch treasure. After she wiped her white fingers on the back of her shorts, she marched, treasure in hand, across the hall and knocked on the door.

Alex's mother welcomed Lucille as the third grader popped into the room, "Who's here, Mom?" Seeing Lucille bearing gifts, he remembered their plans for the afternoon. "Hey, are you ready to run?"

"As a matter of fact I am, Alex, but I brought you a present. Yesterday you gave me a gift."

A puzzled look crossed his face. "You reminded what a good time I had living in this building when I was your age," Lucille began. "That will always be a part of me. Then this morning I was cleaning out the kitchen junk drawer, and I found my mother's recipe for my favorite cookie when I was a kid, Lucy Lemon Bars. Back then my parents called me 'Lucy.' That was before I got so grown up that I had to be called by my given name, Lucille. These cookies are my favorites. My mother would make them for me, and I would wolf down two or three right after she took them out of the oven, warm and buried in that snowy sugar. They remind me of Christmas. So after I got the kitchen all packed up, I found this recipe for my favorite cookies, and I decided to make them for you as a Christmas present."

Alex didn't wait for an invitation. He popped a Lucy Lemon Bar into his mouth and smiled in delight. He reached for another. Alex grinned, and Lucille found herself returning the grin and wondering how she could stuff her mother's glass juicer in her luggage to make Christmas cookies for Bruce.

These cookies are favorites of my granddaughters, none of whom is named Lucy.

Lucy Lemon Bars

Combine the following with a pastry blender:

    1 c. flour

    1/2 c. butter

    1/4 c. powdered sugar

Pat into an eight-by-eight inch baking pan. Bake in a preheated 350-degree oven for 18 to 20 minutes.

Beat 2 large eggs until frothy.

Add the following:

    Zest and juice of one lemon

    1 c. granulated sugar

    1/2 t. baking powder

    1/4 t. salt

Pour over crust and bake for 22 to 25 minutes this time.

When cool, sift powdered sugar on the top.

Cut into 16 squares.

The Present

Growing up on a farm in upstate New York meant our family economy was controlled by the vagaries of the weather, the condition of the farm equipment, the health of the livestock, and the perpetual grind of land taxes paid twice a year. The latter event was always a source of consternation to my father and mother. Frequently there would be heated discussions about expenditures and how to raise the money to keep from tax default. Being the youngest child, I always took these exchanges to heart. I examined my desires and the stresses that I may have placed on our family's always-perilous resources. My peacekeeping tendencies were engrained while I was still in single digits, and I wanted to maintain harmony and to help alleviate that stress to my family's precarious financial condition.

It was a big deal when my older sister and her husband got a new television-stereo combination for Christmas, for we inherited their old TV-radio-stereo combo in the gargantuan mahogany veneer case. We would watch the snowy picture with great intensity. I was appointed to adjust the rabbit ears that sat upon the great box to pull in the three stations in Rochester. On the other side of the console was a stereo player, and the grill cloth below let us hear distinct sounds emanating from the two concealed speakers, a veritable concert in our living room. The stereo had those plastic discs about the size of a half dollar that we could pop into a forty-five-rpm record so we could play the pop hits of the Everly Brothers, Fats Domino, Andy Williams, and Perry Como, who had crooned his way into my mother's heart.

That May a tear-out postcard in the magazine section of the Sunday *Democrat and Chronicle* brought tidings of great joy. If within one year we would buy three records, we would receive three free records. The offer was enticing, and my mother agreed to the deal. I would be brought into the world of Broadway shows and the glories of the Mormon Tabernacle Choir. I would hear Rimsky-Korsakov's *Scheherazade*, Tchaikovsky's *Nutcracker*, Beethoven's soaring Ninth Symphony and the Norman Luboff Choir's dreamy love songs. The seed of music planted when fairies sprinkled the ingredients for life in my mother's forty-year-old womb germinated in that summer of my eleventh year.

But the gift I so treasure came from a very unexpected source—my father. His gift will forever cause me to wonder. Luke the evangelist tells us that Mary kept all the wondrous things of her baby's birth and pondered them in her heart. I have pondered how it was that my father, who darkened the doors of churches only for weddings, baptisms, funerals, and church suppers, would know me so well that his gift would take root and grow to be such a love in my heart.

In July one of the offerings in the Columbia Record Club catalog was a two-disc set of Leonard Bernstein conducting the New York Philharmonic in Handel's *Messiah*. William Warfield was the baritone. Of course it was not a free record. No number of recordings purchased would get you this set. I guess I must have carried that catalog around or talked about it or left it on the dining room table. In August I received a package I hadn't ordered. It was the two-disc set of the *Messiah*.

I was surprised to learn my father had ordered it. I listened to the *Messiah* quite a lot that summer, and come Christmas I listened with my head leaning against the speakers to enjoy the delicious voices standing alone in the arias—the soprano's soothing promise of the Savior bringing peace to the heathen and the alto proclaiming we would be carried like lost lambs when we have strayed from pastures.

But what I couldn't wrap my mind around would come from the Easter section. The soprano sings, "I know that my Redeemer liveth, and that He shall stand at the latter day upon the earth. And though worms destroy this body, yet in my flesh shall I see God (Job 19:25-26, King James Version)." How in the world can your body be destroyed and yet you can still see God? My young mind couldn't comprehend the depth of Job's feelings of abandonment when everything he had given his life to build was destroyed and all that was left was the knowledge that there was no hiding place except with God. It was a divine puzzle, and I pondered it. "Though worms destroy this body, yet in my flesh shall I see God." It was my mantra.

It would be more than thirty years later as I listened again with my heart to the words, for it was then that my marriage lay in ruins and I had no idea of how to repair it. That Christmas the boys and I put the tree up by the fireplace in our basement family room, for my life as I had known it lay about me in pieces like a glass ornament fallen from the tree. I couldn't bear the thought of the tree in its usual center-stage position in the living room. Hidden away, brought to a primal fire in the family room, that was where my Christmas feelings resided that year. I survived. The boys grew, and in time my husband and I were able to put our lives back together. I was never sure if we had pulled a Humpty Dumpty fantasy or if we were standing with the children of Israel in exile, hearing God's words in the midst of their grief, "Behold, I am about to do a new thing; now it springs forth, do you not perceive it?" (Isaiah 43:19).

Another thirty years have passed. My parents and my siblings have all died. This year the *Messiah* brings me great hope. Metaphor rises in the lengthening days of December. The faces of our six grandchildren remind me that though our days are numbered like the hairs on my beloved husband's head, there is this amazing new life running in the midst of the weariness of war and earthquake, poverty and hunger, chasms of greed cracking the once-fertile soil of American democracy, and over-consumption stuffing the corners of loneliness. This Christmas I will see God in my aging flesh and weaker eyes with the wisdom that comes from the journey. It has taken me several decades to unwrap my father's gift and discern what that gift is. Perhaps that is why it is called the present.

By George

She set the tiny package of shells down and began to pick up the strays that the children had used and were still strewn on the sticky table. It is challenging to get six- and seven-year-old fingers to arrange those seashells on the small pieces of molding clay that they had made into pins for their mothers or grandmothers or aunties for Christmas. She smiled at the thought of the conversation and energy of the children at this favorite project every year. She brushed a wisp of gray hair from her face and sat down for a minute at the large craft table to assess the damage. It was always amazing how many shells were still on the table and beneath it, not to mention the craft dough, glue, and spots of paint that were left after those whirlwinds stormed out after Saturday morning's craft class. She smiled as she thought about Holly trying to get every shell possible on her mother's pin. And then George had come in downright hostile when his father had dropped him off.

"Don't take sass from him, Mother. He just got out of the wrong side of the bed," Carol proclaimed with the superiority of being the only eight-year-old who had snuck into the class. But the teacher knew that the wrong side of the bed was a family that was barely making it. Dad was the only parent who struggled with two teenagers who thought "making it" was a walk on the wild side, and George was caught in the detritus of those stormy waters and his father's working two jobs to make ends meet. George sat and fumed for the first ten minutes, and then slowly the fun and joy of the other children busy with their projects lifted his gloom. He started tentatively to put together some shells of various shapes and colors on the molding clay. She wondered to whom he would give his Christmas pin.

A pile of drying craft glue made her chuckle. Mother Phillips remembered T'Shaun and Margaret making a pile of it and burying their shells deeply before putting them on the pin. She could imagine the gooey sensation on their fingers as they plunged the shells into their baptism of Elmer's Craft Glue. Her heart overflowed as she remembered each one of her charges sitting, squirming, and ducking around the two tables pushed together. It was only an hour class, and some of them were there for the vanilla wafers and juice boxes she brought out at ten minutes before the hour to motivate cleaning up and getting their treasures in those little jewelry boxes she had been asking everyone at the community center to save for her in anticipation of the Christmas craft. She knew that those boxes would be delivered as soon as the children found the recipients, for there is something about a gift from a child that has to be given immediately.

She reached down to pick up some shells off the floor. The distance seemed particularly far this morning. "Move it or lose it," she said absentmindedly. Eighty-one years and she was developing the requisite aches of her senior status.

"What are you moving?" a small voice called from the vicinity of the door.

She picked up the shells and turned around to see George leaning against the doorjamb, one sneakered foot on top of the other.

"Why, George, what are you doing here?"

"Waitin,' didn't you notice? He's never on time. Says he has to shop Saturday morning, and he's always late. Don't know why. Never gets stuff I like."

"What do you like, George?"

Was it her tone, her stopping everything and focusing all her energy on him? Maybe it was her merry blue eyes and saying very little that caught the tough seven-year-old off guard.

"I like pancakes. I like hot dogs with ketchup, not mustard. I used to like going to church with Momma, but then she stopped going. Sometimes she would give me cough drops if I got tired of listening to the preacher. I like beating Elroy at basketball and singing in the car when my father used to take us to visit his Momma in Mississippi in the summer. But lately there's not much that I really like."

"Uhm," she said as she found a chair to rest her tired feet. She motioned George toward the other chair that still stood at the table after the stampeding herd with their jewel boxes had thundered out the door. He stood a moment at the door before he decided to accept her wordless invitation. "Where's your jewelry box, George?"

Staring a hole in his sneaker, the boy suddenly seemed so much smaller than his seven years. Letting out a huge sigh he puffed himself up again, and confessed that he had given it to Alisha. She wanted it for her grandmother.

"That was very kind of you. I remember you made a swirling design with your shells that was very pretty. I liked the way the shells were each separate but your design made them all feel like they belonged together," Mother Phillips noted.

He shrugged. "Just threw some shells in the clay. I was angry. My father is always dropping me off and forgetting me. If we didn't live so far out of town, I could've walked."

"I've been angry too, George, a long time ago for a very long time." She now was pushing the boy and his chair a little away from her so she could look him in the eye. A quizzical look shadowed his brow and eyes. "A long time ago … about forty years ago," she continued, "I had a son who was only a couple years older than you, and his big sister was fifteen. She adored him, and they were always doing things together. They loved swimming at Canandaigua Lake. One day in August my son was swimming about fifty feet off shore. All of a sudden a thunderstorm came out of nowhere. George—that was his name too—panicked, and Edna dove in to rescue him. Just as she reached him, there was a deafening clap of thunder and a flash of lightning. My life was changed forever. I lost my children in that storm."

George stole a quick glance at Mother Phillips, who was eyeing him now. "George, I was sad and hurt and angry for the longest time."

"Didn't you have a husband?"

"I did then," Mother Phillips explained, "but about two years later, he died too. I think he died of a broken heart."

George was silent. He stared at his dirty sneaker. He finally spoke. "So what'd you do?"

"I hurt a lot. I felt abandoned by everybody. Then one day I remembered that I still loved art and children very much. I went to Washington, D.C. to live with my sister. She helped me find a job teaching art to children. They were like you, George. Sometimes their families were pretty mixed up and there wasn't a lot of time for the children with all the other things going on."

George's head cocked inquisitively toward the old woman. "Does it get better?"

"It does. Just talking with you for a little while, remembering my son's name was George like yours—it makes me smile inside and out. It's like you today."

"I don't get it," George said.

"Well, we still have to go on. It's tough when you don't feel like it. I can still see you storming in here today, George," Mother Phillips said and chuckled. A knowing smile crossed George's face too. "But Carol reminded you that you weren't the only person here. If I was drawing a cartoon, I would have put a little black cloud over your head. So you just sat there with your arms crossed for a while, and gradually the fun rubbed off on you. Sometimes we just keep going, and we catch a little of the sunshine here and there. When we think about it, the nicest things can happen … like our talking today. I will remember it. You have reminded me of things I really love."

A horn broke the spell. "That's my dad. Good thing he was late today. I like talking to you. Hey, I've got a question. Why does everybody call you 'Mother,' even the parents and old folks?"

She patted his skinny shoulder in departure. "It's strange," she said, walking her charge to the door. "I lost my two children, and when I started back working with children, somehow I became everybody's mother. The name has stuck for forty years. Life's funny, isn't it?"

"See you next week, Mother Phillips," George called, running full tilt to his father. As she headed back to the drying glue, the old woman smiled, knowing her family had grown again today.

An Evening with the Angels

Christmas is for children and the child in each of us. Planning a party for the small children is a wonderful way to step into the magic of Christmas. My first angel party was for children eight and under in a small country church. The children were invited to come in their pajamas. The cold winter night added authenticity to the evening as red-cheeked children squirmed out of jackets, hats, and mittens, some bringing beloved blankets to the party. Older children were invited to come and be helpers for the evening. Neighborhood children, grandchildren, and children at a homeless shelter would also be great guests.

We sang Christmas songs and tried to help our guests learn the words. Then we played "Touched by an Angel." Half the children were seated on one side of the room with their eyes closed, and they had to guess which child from the other side of the room had tapped them with angel wings (hand with fingers tightly together).

We played Jump the Clouds as the children tried to hop over various pillows set up to twist and wind around the room as Christmas carols played. At the end of the trail there was a mattress covered with tons of pillows that the children could jump into with exuberant whoops of joy.

Then the children sat in a tight circle with their legs touching. There were no spaces between the children, legs touching hip to foot. A large ball, one preferably cloud white or sky blue, was tossed into the circle, and with their hands on the floor the children kicked the ball or rolled the ball from one leg to another to keep the angel clouds from falling to earth. After all, it was Christmas. The angels needed those clouds for jumping and hopping! Adults were standing around the outside of the circle to retrieve errant clouds so children could remain in the circle and concentrate on their cloud duties.

After they washed their hands, the children assembled in the kitchen, and each child put four one-and-a-quarter-inch pretzels on paper plates on which their names were written. Then they unwrapped four round caramel Rolo candies and put a candy on top of each of their pretzels. The adults nuked these in the microwave for twenty to thirty seconds until the round candy was soft. Then the children topped the soft candy with a pecan half they smooshed gently into the caramel. The candies were left to cool until time for refreshments.

For this party, a good craft was coffee filter angels. The base, a No.4 natural brown cone coffee filter, folded in two, had a small dot placed exactly in the middle of the folded-over filter. Two paper lace doilies, one four inches and one six inches in diameter, completed the body. The children placed a pencil dot in the center of each doily. A one-and-a-half-inch Styrofoam ball became the angel's head. The body and the head were joined when the filter dot and the two dots on the doilies were aligned, one over the other with the coffee filter underneath. A golf pencil or a short pencil was inserted from the inside of the coffee filter through the three dots halfway into the head. A rubber band had been securely wound around the pencil two inches from the point of the pencil. Elmer's Craft Glue held Spanish moss on the head to resemble hair. The children shaped haloes from four-and-one-half-inch

lengths of yellow pipe cleaners. An inch and one-half piece of florist wire secured the halo to the back of the head. The pajama-clad guests soon proudly displayed their coffee filter angels ready for the trip to each child's home.

Ta-da! It was time for the arrival of the angels. The children were divided into groups of no more than four with a helper for each group. Each group learned that they were to make one of their members into an angel. They received two rolls of paper towels and three rolls of strong-ply toilet tissue to create their angel costumes. After the group angel was dressed, some of the children wanted to dress themselves as angels also. Imagination and fun abounded. We took each group's picture with their angel to e-mail the photo home later or to print as their party favors.

Angels do get hungry. S'mores or another simple snack, angel Christmas cookies, the imitation turtles the children have made, and hot chocolate with marshmallows were waiting at tables decorated with stars on dark blue tablecloths. We reminded the angels of their wonderful manners before eating.

The children gathered in a comfy spot for story time. The mattress covered with pillows was a good landing spot. *The Littlest Angel*, written by Charles Tazewell made a wonderful bedtime story as the party wound down. Older helpers read the story as a radio play for the pint-sized guests as the children imagined a little boy's period of adjustment in becoming an angel. We made sure that the helpers had rehearsed in advance. Good storytelling, rather than reading, can mesmerize children with enthusiastic presentation.

The evening was for everyone who yearned to be a witness to the love that came down at Christmas and brightened our darkest nights and sent pajama-clad guests home to sweet dreams.

Blue Christmas

Christmas isn't for everyone. For some there have been painful losses—a loved one, a job, a home, a divorce—and the thought of gathering with those celebrating is more than they can handle. On the night of the winter solstice, we are reminded of the darkness that enfolds the world and sometimes surrounds us. On or around December 21, many churches pause for a Blue Christmas. Churches are dimly lit, and there are no readings of Christmas scriptures. Instead those who need a time to meditate, remember, and grieve come into a sacred space with quiet music in a dimly lit sanctuary.

Blue Christmas offers the community of accompaniment for those whose hearts are heavy with loss and whose lives are out of sync with the season. Often lay leaders who are involved with the healing ministry of the congregation lead these services. These travelers walk quietly with those who are trying to live with the reality of loss. Music carries the emotion at this service, and it is selected to affirm that a community shares in each loss and that the community, too, is diminished.

Scriptures of comfort with quiet time after each reading carry the intent to be present in the moment. Many unlit candles are at the front of the church, and the invitation is extended to come and light a candle alone or in groups and to name the person or the occasion recalled in this service. A widow came to the Blue Christmas service her church held after her husband died. She just sat there the first year. The second year she leaned over to a man who had a son in prison and said, "I believe I could go up and light a candle and say my husband's name this year. Would you come with me?"

That has been our Advent invitation as we walked to Christmas. We are going to light the candle of our affirmation of God's love, which is still breaking into a weary world. And the invitation of the heartbroken and grieving asks us, "Would you come with us?"

Walking in the Light

If I don't get to Bethl'hem for the breaking of the dawn,

Will you tell those who're gathered that I am moving on?

I am walking in the light now I have pierced the darkest night.

I am walking in the light now, holding fast to God's own hand.

If I didn't see you clearly, if I didn't love you dearly,

Look up. The light still shines. It can flood unyielding lines,

For we're bathed in golden starlight, we are all God's saints in time,

For we're walking in the light now, holding fast to God's own hand.

In the city of mangers, there are no strangers.

We walk by faith and not sight, life's mysteries made bright.

We are free of our obsessions. True joy is our possession.

We are walking in the light now, holding fast to God's own hand.

So on with your journey, we'll meet in the dawn,

For we are the witness that life will be reborn.

We'll look back at the past now, and we'll see God's grand design,

For we're soaring in the light now, wings that bring God's peace divine.

Copyright Elaine Eachus, 2003. Hymn Tune: Natalie Sleeth, "Hymn of Promise."

TLC: Tangled, Loving Circles

A Sermon for the Fourth Sunday in Advent

The autumn clematis is an aggressive garden dweller. From early spring to September its twining tendrils race to every available lattice slant, trellis, or arbor it can find and dance with lightning speed, tendril encircling tendril until its arms hug in a million places. By June no one could ever break them apart, for where they hug each other the two really do seem to "become one flesh." Their intersections are locked tightly. In September the top of this dancing floral climber bursts into a massive, heavenly, cloudlike bloom with an extraordinary fragrance that stirs memories of the lilacs wafting into our windows in May. The tangled vine enfolds our senses as it completes another season. The blossoms are quite unremarkable by themselves, but together heavenly images abound as we are amazed by the working together for glorious good, come September.

Almost Home

We are here at the end of our Advent journey! We have limped, staggered, and wandered, and some resolutely journeyed through Advent to come to Bethlehem. We pause and look into the faces of other limpers, staggerers, wanderers, and pilgrims milling about with us. We are amazed. Most have had difficulty in making the journey. Some were really busy but felt compelled to come. They basically told God that they had places to go and people to meet, yet something lured them. Their faces express surprise that they are here, that they tore themselves away, and that the trip has taught them so many things about themselves. Some faces are marked by a faraway look, as if these people are still searching for the destination. The dreamers sauntered in, listening for long-distance calls and scanning the skies for angel choirs.

If St. Augustine is correct and our souls are restless until they rest in God, then we shouldn't be too surprised that we made the journey each in our own inimitable way. The nature of humankind is that our inklings pull us to find meaning beyond ourselves. Our restless natures mean that we do follow our own drummer and that we will follow our dreams to find our soul's desire. Matthew's gospel tells us that Joseph had a dream in which an angel told him that the child Mary was carrying would be our savior. Joseph was a good man who tried to lead his life to please God. Yet Mary's pregnancy troubled him. He wanted to do what was right, so he answered the angel's command. In Bethlehem, Immanuel was born to Mary and Joseph.

Our Christmas Dream

Was it a dream that brought us here? Or did we come like Ruth came with her mother-in-law, Naomi, just to survive? Maybe in Bethlehem the light is different. Whatever our reason the journey changes us. In Bethlehem we see differently. The restricting contacts that seem to bind and constrain us are in Bethlehem's light, a God-with-us connection. Here we are still a part of a tangled circle with so many points of contact like the autumn clematis. Gathering here, the focus is now on the many, the community gathered by God. Like the astronaut's camera that sent back the first glorious pictures of the earth in space, we are awed when we see through God's wide-angle lens.

When our shoulders were bumping and egos bruised, we weren't able to see that we might have purposes beyond the urge to stretch and be ourselves. We didn't have a clue that those connections were designed to strengthen the community God loves. When we rest in God, we are moving into the deeper knowledge of community. We pilgrims in Bethlehem are catching glimpses of the master plan. In the Gospel John describes Jesus as the Word was with God and was God, coming into being with God. "What has come into being in him was life, and the life was the light of all people. The light shines in the darkness, and the darkness did not overcome it" (John 1:4).

God's Valentine

Soon after my husband and I were married, we bought an antique, four-poster bed. On Valentine's Day that year my husband took yarn and wound it in a tangled web from post to post in a helter-skelter, colorful chaos. There were small gifts on each corner that I had to unravel the yarn to get. I have never forgotten his valentine. It said,

> A tangled web I weave, my love
>
> The object all sublime
>
> The question clear, is this, my dear
>
> Wouldst be my Valentine?

Christmas is God's Valentine to us. Advent journeys twist and turn. They double back and take us from our predetermined, rational courses and whirl us like dervishes until we stagger with disequilibrium. The traveling can get really rough. Leaving home and the familiar is often traumatic. After all, we define ourselves by where we are from. But God's Valentine is in Bethlehem, where we can feel the love God has for his people. How? 1 John 4:7 and 11 tell us,

> Beloved, let us love one another, because love is from God; everyone who loves is born of God and knows God. Whoever does not love does not know God, for God is love. Beloved, since God loved us so much, we also ought to love one another. No one has ever seen God; if we love one another, God lives in us, and his love is perfected in us.

Home for Christmas

In God's geography even the tangles have the potential to lead to love. The knots can show us the how-to of loving. The patience to untie a tangled mass or to try to envision new ways of working things out means we can change into those persons beloved of God, who have never seen God but acknowledge that God lives in us, as God lives in everyone. Advent Pilgrims have honored their restlessness and have backed away from the glimmering enticements of the culture. It has taken courage. It takes a gigantic leap of faith to be willing to drift in the sea of too many choices until the light shines in our darkness. Then we can chart our course.

In Bethlehem we find TLC, tangled, loving circles. They hold us in an intertwining community, bound in love. They hold us so that we may see God's glory, grace, and truth, and in turn may live that Word in our lives. We share in the joy of God breaking into humanity. And here in Bethlehem, in the beloved community of pilgrims, the Word shapes us for God's purposes. Like the shepherds who came off the Judean hillsides on a star-filled night, we will see Immanuel, God-with-us, and return home glorifying and praising God. Pilgrims in future time will see our blooming, like the autumn clematis in the tangled, interconnected circles and will marvel at the power of the Holy Child to bring us to the place where peace and righteousness kiss. Amen.

The Sled

Estelle was a child of the depression several years after the depression was officially over. Indeed, Estelle was born early in the morning. Her father was milking the cows while his wife brought forth another girl (of all things) and unceremoniously brought her home to dwell in the hardscrabble life of too much work and not enough hands to make a decent living on their farm. Certainly it would have been better of this oops child, born when her mother was almost forty-one, had been a boy. Then at least there would have been another farmhand to help her father. As it was, there was only one boy and three girls on the farm nestled in the hills of the lake country.

Estelle, which means star, was God's child. She loved the animals of the farm; she loved the flowers that her mother would nurture with the manure she lugged from the cow stable. She loved the breeze in her hair when she and her dog would ride on the back of her father's truck. She loved helping on the farm. You could count on Estelle to be a good girl. She did what she was told. She minded her manners, a very important social skill if you were going to be poor. She loved to read, skipping kindergarten to get into the good stuff of first grade a little early.

Despite a cold, drafty farmhouse, she found joy in making what they did have look good. She dutifully arranged the secondhand and hand-me-down furniture in the living room on Saturdays. She brought snow in to sweep the threadbare living room rugs. She polished the stained furniture and tried to be her mother's helper. She strove for her father's affection too! She would drive the tractor in June as he picked up the heavy bales of first-cutting of alfalfa, and in late July they picked up straw, the residue from the oats and wheat. She would bring him cups of instant coffee laced with two scoops of sugar and cream from their cows in those thick, scratched, white coffee mugs of the fifties.

And Estelle had a secret weapon. It was her aunt. Aunt Alice, a kindergarten teacher, lived with the family during the summers and school vacations. Aunt Alice never married. She paid for Estelle's piano lessons. Aunt Alice bought the farm children some of the things that couldn't be paid for out of the small milk check, which was the only regular income the family had. Aunt Alice had a secret too, although Estelle didn't know it for more than fifty years. Her aunt would somehow manage to get a dress for Estelle's piano recital or the money for a class ring her junior year in high school, and when it came to college, Aunt Alice helped Estelle to become the first member of her family to get a four-year college education.

It happened when she was in second grade. Christmas was coming, and Estelle knew what that meant. In the cold winter afternoons of December her mother would head upstairs to her treadle sewing machine, and as the bobbin and needle did their rhythmic dance between layers of soft, warm "outing flannel," as her mother called it, nightgowns and pajamas would be made for every member of the family. It was fun to stroke the soft yellows and blues of the cloth on Christmas morning when the family opened their presents after their father did the morning milking. Like most farm routines, Christmas was pretty predictable for Estelle. Her brother and two older sisters would get their pajamas, and she would get a nightgown. Her father would get a striped nightshirt. During good years the family would also get a pair of bedroom slippers. During very good years everyone would find a hardly folded five-dollar bill inside the soft fabric. Aunt Alice would add to the festivities as she would repurpose various gifts her kindergarten children had given her for her nephew and nieces. Jewelry and candy were the most likely gifts.

There was also a tradition that the youngest child would give out the gifts Christmas morning as soon as he or she could read, so she had been the Santa for a couple years. This year seemed like a no-brainer.

Her older siblings, who were now twelve, fifteen, and seventeen, dealt with Christmas with adolescent disinterest, although they still were hopeful that this year would bring clothes instead of pajamas or at least something to show off when they went back to school after Christmas vacation. Without a great deal of anticipation the family gathered in the large living room where Estelle and her mother had installed the large pine tree they had cut from a neighbor's lot. It was a little tipsy that year, so they tied it to the window latch to prevent a catastrophe. Estelle loved putting on the lights. There was something about the scent of pine, the large multicolored lights of green, blue, red, yellowy gold, and white that made her heart dance. She cleaned the room, lovingly brought out the Christmas decorations from the back of the closet, and cranked up the radio, listening for Christmas carols to fill her heart with charm and possibility. She baked Christmas cookies, for by now she had mastered the sugar cookie recipe, and she rolled stars, candy canes, trees, and ornaments. Christmas was all about hope for the seven-year-old heart. Being jaded, she decided, came with age, as her siblings ignored her Christmas preparations. This year she was doing her part for the miracle to come to life.

There was the Christmas party at school where you brought fifty-cent gifts for a grab bag. Even for Estelle in second grade, this was one of the more disappointing aspects of the holiday. She never got something she considered useful, and she was a pragmatic child. Aunt Alice came for Christmas vacation.

The Christmas Eve pageant at church was a different story. Here Hollywood could not touch the depth of realism she felt as the boys dressed in their plaid flannel bathrobes walked down the drafty aisles of the church, and the small congregation sang, "While Shepherds Watched Their Flocks by Night." Her heart erupted with joy as the "Silent Night" candles turned the tiny sanctuary into Mary's maternity ward and God's redemption center.

The next morning after her father came in from milking, the family assembled in the sunny living room. Her mother had made sweet rolls and fried bacon, which she kept warm on the woodstove in the kitchen. Breakfast would be a feast after the gifts were opened.

Estelle waited until her father came in and sat down. Then methodically she delivered the presents, making sure everybody got one present before she would start the second round. She was anxious to see her father's reaction to the flannel shirt she had gotten him. Aunt Alice had bought a bird book for her sister. Estelle herself had made an apron for Aunt Alice. Her mother had helped her with gathering the waistband and doing most of the sewing. Still Estelle was pretty proud of her first endeavor for the aunt who made her feel important and noticed what was important to the youngest child. Her sisters and brothers had gotten each other presents this year, and they were pretty impressed with the gear they had accumulated. Her lanky, six-foot, twelve-year-old brother got a pair of leather gloves, her fifteen-year-old sister received an angora sweater, and her oldest sister received a red blouse, her favorite color, with mother-of-pearl buttons down the front and on the cuffs.

Gifts distributed, Estelle sat down at her small pile. She opened her nightie, which had yellow, blue-striped, blue, and green-striped panels. (Hers was made from the material left over from the other sleepwear her mother had sewn.) Her slippers this year were moccasins—red with white fur around the ankle and a few Indian beads sewn around the toe. She received Lois Lenski's book *Strawberry Girl* and a deck of canasta cards. She could imagine playing canasta when the cousins would gather later in the week. Her siblings gave her a fuzzy white muff with a small purse sewn into the back. She thought that would impress the girls in Sunday School. She knew her mother would never let her carry that to school.

Estelle's thoughts wandered off to breakfast when she noticed everyone in the room was watching her. "Estelle should have gotten glasses for Christmas," her father said, leaving Estelle embarrassed for what she might have omitted. She looked from face to face; everyone was looking at the girl whose mind was racing, as she never liked to be left out.

"Estelle," Aunt Alice began, "Have you delivered all the presents?" Red-faced, she scanned the tree for a box that might have been placed in the boughs. Nothing. She walked around as much of the tree as she could. It had been tied tight to the window latch to keep it vertical. Then she saw the final present pressed against the wall, hidden by the branches of the tree. Laughing, she pulled the sled out from its den and smoothed the silver runners and noted the red logo and lettering on the wooden slats. She had never recalled anybody in her family ever receiving such a frivolous, impractical gift. She couldn't believe her eyes. It was a gift beyond imagining. It was a source of years of joy as she rode the slippery, icy roads of the hills around her parents' farm.

Estelle is a grandmother now, but every Christmas Estelle drags out an old sled with the handles held on with duct tape, runners rusty. She tops it with a Christmas wreath to welcome the season when love breaks in and surprises us with the gift beyond imagination. And Estelle's secret—well, it took her years to even question it and another fifty years or so to figure it out. The pieces came together when she was visiting Aunt Alice in the nursing home. It was just a chance remark from her aunt as they were reminiscing. Aunt Alice said, "I wanted you to slide through life and enjoy the ride." After Aunt Alice died, Estelle thought about the remark and began to put things together. Aunt Alice had seen Estelle for who she was, a rather lonely child who was often picked on by her brother and sisters, and the sled was a gift that would bring joy to her. Nobody else in the family was at an age to be interested in it. So at Christmas if someone doesn't thank you for your gift, don't despair. Estelle is still saying thank you sixty years after her amazing gift. Thanksgiving does lead to Christmas.

Long Ago Star

The star that shone so long ago shines in my heart tonight.

My path is far from Bethlehem still well I know its sight.

My journey's far away from home, familiar things I've known.

Yet I'm compelled by star-bright beams for home's not what it seems.

For I've walked down the broad highway, convinced of my control.

I sought as others walking there, and tried the world to hold.

But songs and stars and mysteries speak language seldom known.

And all I had, possessed, and owned, turned cold, as cold as stone.

Star beams, dark thoughts and agony dwelt in this silent heart.

I walked a path, alone, afraid; my dreams had fallen apart.

In deserts new visions arise; silence shouts aloud.

On lonely steps our hearts are cheered by hosts: the silent crowd.

It dawns, it shines, it sings, it shouts. It makes the struggle right.

For I possess the light that shone for Jesus Christ that night.

My joy no words can yet describe, my spirit starts to thrive.

It's God who guides our questing hearts to life so newly alive.

Words and music copyright, Elaine Eachus, 2013

Long Ago Star

Words & Music by Elaine Eachus
Arranged by Louise Brodie

Soprano

The star that shone so long a - go, shines in my he-art to
For I've walked down the broad high - way, con - vinced of my __ con-

night. My __ path is far from Beth - le - hem still well I
trol. I __ sought as o - thers walk - ing there, and tried the

know __ its sight. My jour - ney's far a - way from home, fa -
world __ to hold. But songs and stars and mys - ter - ies speak

mil - iar things I've known. Yet I'm com - pelled by star - bright
lan - guage sel - dom known. And all I had, po - sessed and

beams for home's not what __ it seems
owned, turned cold, as cold __ as stone.

Star beams, dark thoughts and agony dwelt in this silent heart.
I walked a path, alone, afraid; my dreams had fallen apart.
In deserts new visions arise; silence shouts aloud.
On lonely steps our hearts are cheered by hosts: the silent crowd.

It dawns, it shines, it sings, it shouts. It makes the struggle right.
For I possess the light that shone for Jesus Christ that night.
My joy no words can yet describe, my spirit starts to thrive.
It's God who guides our questing hearts to life so newly alive.

Lullaby for Christmas

Little boy, little boy, sleep, my baby, sleep.

We saw the star, it shone so bright,

We started out, glorious night!

Little boy, little boy, sleep, my baby, sleep.

Cold was the night, silent the road.

Following, awed, the star path showed.

Little boy, little boy, sleep, my baby, sleep.

Bethlehem's town, easily found,

Dark streets and inns, the search begins.

Strange how God gives us a new way to go.

Things thought so mighty, now are brought low.

Here in this stable away from the crowd.

Peasant and child, no king for the proud.

Yet in my heart on this holy, clear night

A sleeping child makes my heart right

My step grows sure and my heart, it grows brave,

God's precious child asleep in the cave.

Little boy, little boy, sleep, my baby, sleep.

Jesus, no wonder we all come this way:

beauty and joy you give us today.

We're changed, we're shaped by the lure of the star.

Jesus, we come and kneel where you are.

Little boy, little boy, sleep, my baby, sleep.

Lu, lu, lu, lu, lu.

Words and music copyright, Elaine Eachus, 2013

Long Ago Star

Words & Music by Elaine Eachus

Arranged by Louise Brodie

Soprano

The star that shone so long a - go, shines in my he-art to
For I've walked down the broad high - way, con - vinced of my __ con-

night. My __ path is far from Beth - le - hem still well I
trol. I __ sought as o - thers walk - ing there, and tried the

know __ its sight. My jour - ney's far a - way from home, fa -
world __ to hold. But songs and stars and mys - ter - ies speak

mil - iar things I've known. Yet I'm com - pelled by star - bright
lan - guage sel - dom known. And all I had, po - sessed and

beams for home's not what __ it seems
owned, turned cold, as cold __ as stone.

Star beams, dark thoughts and agony dwelt in this silent heart.
I walked a path, alone, afraid; my dreams had fallen apart.
In deserts new visions arise; silence shouts aloud.
On lonely steps our hearts are cheered by hosts: the silent crowd.

It dawns, it shines, it sings, it shouts. It makes the struggle right.
For I possess the light that shone for Jesus Christ that night.
My joy no words can yet describe, my spirit starts to thrive.
It's God who guides our questing hearts to life so newly alive.

Lullaby for Christmas

Little boy, little boy, sleep, my baby, sleep.

We saw the star, it shone so bright,

We started out, glorious night!

Little boy, little boy, sleep, my baby, sleep.

Cold was the night, silent the road.

Following, awed, the star path showed.

Little boy, little boy, sleep, my baby, sleep.

Bethlehem's town, easily found,

Dark streets and inns, the search begins.

Strange how God gives us a new way to go.

Things thought so mighty, now are brought low.

Here in this stable away from the crowd.

Peasant and child, no king for the proud.

Yet in my heart on this holy, clear night

A sleeping child makes my heart right

My step grows sure and my heart, it grows brave,

God's precious child asleep in the cave.

Little boy, little boy, sleep, my baby, sleep.

Jesus, no wonder we all come this way:

beauty and joy you give us today.

We're changed, we're shaped by the lure of the star.

Jesus, we come and kneel where you are.

Little boy, little boy, sleep, my baby, sleep.

Lu, lu, lu, lu, lu.

Words and music copyright, Elaine Eachus, 2013

Lullaby for Christmas

Words and Music by Elaine Eachus

Arranged by Louise Brodie

Soprano

Lit-tle boy,____ lit-tle boy,____ sleep, my ba-by sleep.____ We saw the star, it shone so bright, we start-ed out glor-i-ous____ night!____ Lit-tle boy,____ lit-tle boy,____ sleep, my ba-by sleep.____ Cold was the night, si-lent the road. Fol-low-ing, awed, the star____ path showed____ Lit-tle boy,____ ____ lit-tle boy,____ sleep, my ba-by sleep.____ Beth-le-hem's town, ea-si-ly found, dark streets and inns, the search____ be-gins.____ ____ Strange how God gives us a new way to go. Things thought so

©2013

59

57 might-y, now are brought low. Here in this sta-ble, a - way from the

63 crowd. Pea-sant and child, no king for the proud._____ Yet in my

70 heart on this ho - ly, clear night a sleep - ing child makes my heart

76 right. My step grows sure and my heart, it grows brave. God's pre-cious

82 child a - sleep in the cave._____ Lit - tle boy,_____ lit - tle boy,_____

90 sleep, my ba - by sleep._____ Je - sus, no won-der we all come this

97 way; beau - ty and joy you give us to - day. We're changed, we're

103 shaped by the lure of the star. Je - sus we come and kneel where you are.

110 Li - tle boy,_____ lit - tle boy_____ sleep my ba - by sleep____

118 ____ Lu, lu lu lu lu_____

Edwards Brothers Malloy
Oxnard, CA USA
October 4, 2013